Lauren copies out the essay-title. She turns round to see Jason staring at her. 'Oh no, don't watch me . . . it's no good Jason, you've got to go.'

'What have I done now?'

'Nothing, it's just . . .' Her bedroom door bursts open and her dad is suddenly glowering in front of them. He strides over to Jason, grabs hold of his shirt collar and pulls him to his feet. Then he roars, 'When my daughter's studying for her exams, you are banned from this house.' He starts jabbing Jason's neck with his fingers. 'Banned, do you understand?'

Jason doesn't reply. He doesn't even seem to have heard what her father's said. He just stares fixedly ahead of him. Then, Jason starts brushing his collar down, with what teachers used to call 'an insolent smile' on his face. He strolls to the door. Lauren calls out his name but he doesn't look back.

Pete Johnson has a panel of readers across the country who are the first to see his books. Here are their comments on *Everything Changes*.

'EVERYTHING CHANGES. *How appropriate that title is. It perfectly sets off the best book of the series. Some of the scenes were the most touching I've ever read and maybe will read. Jez came back and about time too. Wasn't he great, always the joker but with feelings as deep, if not deeper than anyone else. Cathy's still a favourite with me, just as she was in Book One.*'

'*This book moved me so much, maybe because I really believed what was going on. It was very true to life, especially the scenes between Adam and Becky. The ending was a surprise and yet I liked it very much. If all your future books are as good as this one, you'll have no trouble selling them.*'

'*All the characters are good but Jason is the standout. I like the way we see a little more of him in each book, but in this one we go right behind his mask. He's funny too: a wicked character.*'

PETE JOHNSON

FRIENDS FOREVER 4

EVERYTHING
CHANGES

Teens · Mandarin

First published in Great Britain 1992
by Teens . Mandarin
an imprint of Mandarin Paperbacks
Michelin House, 81 Fulham Road, London SW3 6RB

Mandarin is an imprint of Reed Consumer Books Ltd

ISBN 0 7497 0650 3

A CIP catalogue record for this title
is available from the British Library

Printed in Great Britain
by Cox & Wyman Ltd, Reading, Berkshire

This book is dedicated to those special friends, whose generous spirit and wicked sense of fun mark them out as my (I hope!) 'friends forever'.

JAN, LINDA, ROBIN BIRCH, HILARY LAPEDIS, GILL PARSONS, MARTIN HEFFRON, GINNY MARTIN, BILL BLOOMFIELD, LISA FARRON, ASHLEY NOBLE, DANEEN MOWAT, JO MELLER, ROSE JEWITT and DARREN RUMBLE, who let ADAM borrow a few lines from his brilliant poem, 'Deepwater Kiss'.

'Friendship, another shared dream, something the participants have to believe in and put their faith in, trusting that it will go on forever.'

Raymond Carver

Contents

	Letter from Mark	ix
1	Becky's Dilemma	1
2	A Trip to Downing Street – and Shock News	17
3	Mark's Brilliant Plan	39
4	Stolen From the Post	64
5	An Election and an Emergency	71
6	Thomas	95
7	'I Don't Fancy You Anymore'	108
8	'I Want You to Come With Me'	140
9	'Friends Forever'	177

17, Wheeler Avenue
CARTFORD

Yo!

Mark, here! How's things? I thought I'd drop you a few lines to fill you in on the latest news. And a lot's been happening.

The *Friends Forever* books star Jason, Cathy, Adam, Jez, Becky, Lauren and yours truly. We've been friends for years and we look out for each other. Now we're at college, except for Jason, who works at the local sports shop, and Jez – I honestly don't know what he's doing. I hope he does. He's dossing abroad somewhere. Cathy gets the occasional postcard or phone call.

I'm sure that exciting information has improved your life. Now for the juicy bits. Lauren and Jason are going out together again (at last) but they've just had a big row. They were going to this party at the college, only Jason made Lauren change her dress. He thought it was far too short! Then, at the party, Jason thought Lauren was spending too much time with two guys from her English class and he walked out.

Meanwhile, Cathy's had problems, number one being Giles. This is her mum's boyfriend. Giles is going to marry Cathy's mum, so now Cathy's walked out and is staying at Lauren's. Cathy also went to the party but later on she was in Cartford town centre, hurling a stone through a butcher's window. She did this in a moment of frustration (she thinks killing animals for meat is wrong). Anyway, who should turn up but Jason – and a few seconds later, the police. And yes, Jason tells the police it was he who smashed the window and is hauled off to the police station. What a gentleman!

You're probably wondering where I was all this time, (you are, aren't you!) Well, I was supposed to be boogieing at the party with my great friend, Becky (who I fancy like crazy, Cartford's worst kept secret). She is going out with Adam, much to his parents' displeasure, for they are strict Jews and only want him to become serious about another Jewish girl. Anyway, I was escorting Becky to the party (Adam was working), but I sensed she was really upset about something. Then I said, and it was just a wild guess, 'You're not pregnant, are you?' – and she thinks she is. I said she's got to find out. So I'm going down the clinic with her this morning. I'm the only one who knows Becky's secret and it's quite a responsibility. I feel a bit out of my depth, to tell the truth.

x

Shall we rush on to the next page? Yeah, let's go. See you there. Look after yourself.

Mark

Becky's Dilemma

'To be honest, Mark, I don't know how I feel,' says Becky. 'It's funny, while I was waiting at the clinic, my head was buzzing but as soon as they said, "Yes, your test is positive," I just went numb. And I could hear this woman gabbling away, giving me all this advice and I was being so calm, because I wasn't there at all, really. And I still feel so strange.'

'Do you want any more tea?' asks Mark.

'No, thanks.'

'How about something to eat?'

'No, I'm fine. Stop fussing.' They're in their favourite café. On the window-ledge opposite, a wasp is decomposing, while at the table next to them is one of the regulars, an oldish guy with wisps of hair the colour of digestive biscuits. He sits with his paper propped up against a mug of

1

tea, wolfing down a plateful of chips. That's all he eats, chips. Mark dubbed him, 'The Cholesterol King'. He nods at Becky. She smiles back. She and Mark know most of the faces in here. How often has she sat in here with nothing more important to worry about than tonight's homework?

But now, suddenly, she is not alone. How absurd that phrase sounds: she is not alone. And yet, even as she sits here . . . a life within a life. Inside her world another world is forming. What is she to do? It's such a serious question, she can only bear to ask it as a kind of joke. 'So Mark, what am I going to do?'

He replies gravely. 'You've got to consider all the options.'

'Yes, I know. But what do you think?'

Mark sits back. 'Only you can decide. I can't say, can I?'

'No.' She hesitates. 'I could keep my baby, couldn't I?'

'Yes, you could,' says Mark, cautiously.

'Girls younger than me have kept babies. There was this girl at my old school, Rachel, she had a baby before she was fifteen and she was just so chuffed about it all.' She pauses. 'Mark, do you want to hear something dreadful?'

'Always.'

She smiles. 'While I was waiting for the result, deep down, a part of me really wanted the test to be

2

"Yes". And even now, a part of me, the unrealistic part, can't help thinking how wonderful to have a baby of my own.' Her voice is barely above a whisper now. 'Mark, I want this baby so much.'

Mark doesn't quite know what to say to that. Somehow, he'd assumed she would get rid of it. That's what she should do, isn't it? Not that he can tell her to do that. But somehow, he can't see Becky turning into someone like his sister, who seems to be joined at the hip to her two children, his little nieces. His sister, who always smells of baby powder and Farley's rusks. Could that be Becky in a few months' time? Mark can't see that at all. But then, his sister's twenty-six, nearly ten years older than Becky.

Becky goes on. 'Shortly before I moved here I met Rachel in the town centre. She was a year older than me at school, so she'd have been about seventeen then, and to be honest, she looked more like thirty-seven, no exaggeration. I mean, she used to be quite pretty but her skin had gone all greasy and her hair was straggly.'

'But that won't happen to you,' interrupts Mark, quickly.

'Maybe, maybe not. And then when I saw Rachel, there was this guy standing behind her, she introduced me to him as her other half, and he just looked so totally bored by her and the baby. I thought, he won't be around much longer. He's not ready for all that responsibility. One day soon, he'll leave and then it will be just Rachel, all on her own. I felt so sorry for her and yet, in a way, I despised her too, for messing up her life. And now, I've . . .' She covers her face with her hand and starts to sob quietly. Then she glances up and sees Mark looking at her with such an anxious expression, that she whispers, 'I'm sorry.'

'No, you're all right . . . and you're not on your own. You've got me and Cathy – and everyone.' Then he adds, 'And your mum.'

'My mum,' she shakes her head. 'I can't not tell her.'

Mark says, 'Do you know what I thought was weird today: at that family planning clinic there were only women waiting. There wasn't one bloke in the place, apart from me. That's not right, is it? After all, they've played a part in it.'

'So you think I should tell Adam next?'

Actually, Mark hadn't been thinking of Adam. And there's a part of him that would rather Adam didn't know, why not keep it a secret from him? For once Adam is told, Mark's back to being a very minor character, isn't he? Yet, Adam's the father.

'I suppose you should tell Adam,' he says, glumly.

'Yes,' says Becky. 'I must tell Adam first.'

*

4

'Hey, Jason, broken any windows lately?' The guy coming towards Jason is grinning away at him. What's his name? Jason's forgotten. All he remembers about this guy is that he's a peanut head. So Jason doesn't even reply, just gives the guy a quick wink and walks on towards the sports centre.

Still, he reflects, news travels fast in Cartford, doesn't it? Funny, to think less than twelve hours ago he was sitting in a police station, watching his parents bursting a few blood vessels. His dad went bellowing on about how Jason couldn't take the law into his own hands and how he'd got a criminal record now. His dad hasn't said so much to him for years. Then he declared he was washing his hands of Jason. Jason said, he thought his dad had done that already. His mum just kept babbling the same things, like a mad woman: 'I don't understand why you did it. I'm trying to but I can't,' to which Jason replied, 'Fair enough.' What else could he say? 'Actually, Mum, I did it for a girl, the nicest girl I know.' He grins at the idea of saying anything so personal to his parents. Then he smiles again, as he pictures Cathy standing by that smashed window, looking scared witless yet eerily beautiful, too. She looked like Cathy and yet she didn't.

First thing this morning Cathy was on the phone to him in the shop, saying how she couldn't let him take the blame for last night. She was pretty sweet actually, all breathy and concerned. But Jason just

5

said, 'It's sorted and there's absolutely nothing to worry about.'

And there wasn't really. The police had asked him a lot of questions about all the other 'animal rights activists'. They were the ones the police were after. Jason, of course, said nothing. And finally the police gave up on him and said he could expect a letter telling him when he had to appear in court. The word 'court' did give Jason a few twinges, but only for a second. Then it was back to thinking about much more important matters: Lauren.

What's she doing now? Meeting those two guys from her English group for coffee? Having a nice intellectual chat about some crappy new book of sixteenth-century love poetry or something?

He really fouled up last night, didn't he? It was just seeing the way those two plebs were looking at Lauren knocked everything else out of his head. Even now it's pounding furiously. It's obvious to anyone with half a brain that those two guys do fancy Lauren. But Lauren only fancies Jason. Or she did. Girls change, don't they, and usually when you're least expecting it? It can all be so great and then . . . you can't hold on to it. That's what makes going out with a girl so stressful. You've got to keep proving to yourself that she still cares.

Now he's walking into the sports centre. Despite feeling rough, he'll go to his usual weight-training session as that's one time when his head starts buzzing with ideas. He's got to work out a grovelly apology. After that, he and Lauren will go back to where they were before, won't they?

Cathy takes a deep sniff, 'Mmm, I love the smell of red roses, it seems to go somewhere deep inside me. I'll put this in water, if you like, Lauren.'

'I can do that, Cathy,' says Lauren.

'No, it's all right.' Cathy likes doing little jobs while she's staying with Lauren.

Cathy gives Jason a quick smile before disappearing out of the lounge, leaving Lauren fingering the note which had accompanied the rose. In red capitals he'd scrawled, SORRY. Underneath were some kisses, in the shape of hearts.

Jason gives a sly smile. 'You can put that card with all my other ones.'

Lauren can feel her lips twisting too. 'I'll need a special drawer soon.'

'The Jason Apology Drawer,' he's laughing now. It's all a big joke and now he's gliding over to the sofa, sprawling himself across it.

Lauren watches him, thinking it's not really sorted. He'll become jealous again and then what? More cards and flowers. He thinks that solves everything, doesn't he? Jason knows she'll forgive him every time. How weak that makes her sound, like one of those girls who are totally dominated

7

by their boyfriends, who never go anywhere, in fact, without their boyfriends coming too.

But that's not Lauren. She's still going with Russell and Damian to the play. They were quite amazed when she told them. 'Doesn't he mind?' they asked. 'It's not up to him,' replied Lauren, firmly.

Cathy returns with a tray of coffee and chocolate biscuits, just as the telephone rings in the hallway. Lauren hears her mother say, 'Yes, she is, who is it please?' Then her mother opens the lounge door and says, 'Excuse me, Lauren, you're wanted on the phone.' It is only when Lauren closes the door that her mum hisses, 'It's a boy, someone called Russell.' Suddenly, Lauren wants to laugh. Her mum looks as if she's in a spy film, passing on secret information.

'It's okay, Mum. It's just a boy in my English class.' She picks up the receiver. 'Hi, Russell.'

There's a pause. 'Lauren, I just rang up to say I've booked us tickets in the stalls.'

'Fine.'

'The only thing is, Damian can't make it after all.'

There's a silence.

'So it'll be just you and me,' purrs Lauren.

'Yes.'

Lauren laughs to herself. They've planned this

between themselves, of course. It's almost sweet. 'That'll be cosy, won't it?' she says.

Now Russell can hardly speak he's so excited, and Lauren's really enjoying herself. This will show Jason, and everyone else, what kind of person she is. Did she really change her dress last night, just because Jason thought it was too short? Guess what dress she'll be wearing to the theatre?

Back in the lounge Jason is asking Cathy, 'So you reckon Lauren's pretty happy about everything now?'

'I'm sure she is,' says Cathy. 'I still feel bad though, about last night and the way you . . .'

'Stop babbling.' Jason waves a dismissive hand. 'Look, we're friends, we look out for each other, there's no need for any of that other stuff. That just devalues it.'

'All right, but I want to say, I'll never forget the way you dived in and took the blame for me. It was so . . . Sometimes, you make a kamikaze pilot look cautious.'

Jason laughs out loud at this. He obviously liked that. Then, he says, 'You made me see you a bit differently last night.'

'I did? How?' asks Cathy, silently praying that Lauren won't come back in yet.'

'I always see you,' says Jason, 'as an old soul.'

'Oh,' squeaks Cathy. That doesn't sound very flattering.

'What I mean is, some people seem to be born knowing what to do, they never make any massive mistakes, they don't seem to have to go through things. They know, already, as if they've been here before: that's what I mean by an old soul.'

'I see,' said Cathy. It still doesn't make her sound very exciting.

'But last night you went crazy, didn't you, and I saw you in a whole new way.' Is that why you kissed me? wonders Cathy. Why did you kiss me? How she'd love to ask him. It meant so much and yet, every time she thinks about it, she feels as if she's letting Lauren down. That's why she must forget it. She asks, 'So are you an old soul, too?'

Jason considers this and then his tone becomes unexpectedly confiding. 'Now, I'm what you call a swing personality. One day I'm convinced I've lived many times before, because I know so much and I'm just so wise. Then, other days, I'm stuck with this young soul who knows nothing and I just make one foul-up after another.'

Lauren comes back in then and he swiftly changes the subject. But Cathy's already storing away everything he said to her. And tonight she'll annoy herself by lying awake and running over every single word.

'Are you sure you're not in a draught there?' asks Adam.

10

'No, I'm fine, honestly,' replies Becky.

'It's just you look really cold.'

He sounds so concerned. Becky's touched and yet irritated too, without knowing why. 'I'm fine,' she repeats shortly. Actually, she's a long way from fine. She woke up shivering and she just can't seem to get warm today.

Adam has brought her to The Anchor for a pub lunch. It's just outside the town centre. It's a cosy pub with an open fire and little clusters of comfortable chairs and sofas. Only the lunches haven't arrived yet and Adam has got a class in twenty minutes.

'You're going to have to go soon,' says Becky.

'It's okay,' says Adam. 'It's only Bailey. He just goes, "Good evening", if you're late.'

'Yes, but they said quick service on the door. They shouldn't write that if it's not true.' She's feeling crabby and ratty and washed-out. She looks up to see the meal's finally arriving: fish and chips for Adam, baked potato with tuna for her. Becky starts poking her potato with a fork, then she lets out a cry of annoyance. 'This is raw in the middle, solid. I can't eat this.'

Adam looks up. 'Are you sure?'

'Yes, this hasn't been cooked properly.'

'Do you want me to send it back?'

'There isn't time.'

'Can't you eat round the edges?'

11

'No, no, it's okay, I'll just have the rabbit food.' She starts eating the salad. Adam slings a pile of chips on to her plate.

'Adam, it's all right.'

'No, go on, I can't eat all these anyway.' He sits back on his chair and groans. 'I've just remembered, I'm supposed to be handing in homework today. Well, I haven't done it.' He starts eating again. 'Maybe my mum's right, I am getting lazy.'

Becky smiles. 'Is that what she said?'

'Oh, yeah, she gave me this big lecture about how I wasn't applying myself. She goes, you're trying to do it all and you can't. You've plenty of time to go out with girls after you've finished your exams.'

Becky stops smiling. 'What exactly did she mean by that?'

Adam looks embarrassed. 'Oh, you know my mum.'

'Yes,' says Becky flatly. 'And she's blaming me for you not working.'

'Afraid so,' says Adam lightly. Then he adds, 'Eat your chips and forget it.'

But Becky doesn't do either of these things. Instead, she suddenly feels choked up with anger and frustration and tiredness. How dare Adam's mum blame her? Why does she always have to take insults from Adam's family? Nothing she does is ever right.

12

'You look well-annoyed now,' says Adam, and there's a nervous edge to his voice.

Becky doesn't answer.

'I shouldn't have told you,' says Adam.

'I'd rather know,' says Becky shortly.

'You're really upset, aren't you?' asks Adam.

Becky doesn't answer this. But deep inside herself she lets out a great howl of pain. Suddenly, she just feels so miserable and far away from everyone, even Adam. Especially Adam. And she can't sit freezing to death in this pub another minute.

'Have you finished?' she asks. 'Otherwise, you're going to be late.' She gets up while Adam is still gobbling down his chips. As they pass the bar Becky shouts, 'My potato wasn't cooked properly, it was all raw in the middle!' She wouldn't normally have said this, but right now there's so much anger in her, it can't help bursting out.

The woman behind the counter doesn't look as if she's one for holding back either and she cries, 'There's no need to shout it out like that.'

'Why isn't there?' says Becky. 'It's the truth.' Now the woman looks as if she'd like to pull Becky across the bar.

'The potato wasn't cooked properly,' says Adam quietly.

'If you'd asked me nicely you could have had another one,' she says.

'I never want to eat in here again,' cries Becky,

trembling with rage. But she lets herself be propelled to the door by Adam.

Outside, Becky is saying, 'Horrible place, horrible.' Then she adds, 'You'd better go.'

'No, I can't leave you like this.'

'Like what?'

'All upset.'

'I'm not upset.' He touches her arm but she pulls away. 'Go to your class,' she says.

'No way.'

'You must. Can't have your mum blaming me for that too.' And right now, she really does want Adam to go away as fast as he can and never come back. She wants him out of her life. It's the best thing anyway. Since they met, it's been nothing but hassle and grief.

He stares at her, anxious, confused, not knowing what to say. 'Becky, I'm not in the mood for going to a lesson now, it'll be really boring anyway . . .'

But Becky is already walking away. 'Adam, as a favour to me, just go to your lesson. Please.' She shrieks the last word before almost running into the park, the wind whirling behind her. She finally turns round, expecting him to be still standing there. But he's gone. She's never going to see him again. She's free, at last.

She'll go away. Mark will help her to have a secret abortion and then start a new life. *Her life.* For since she's gone out with Adam, she's lost

14

herself. All she's really thought about is him. Where has that got her? Absolutely nowhere. And look at the mess she's in now. Still, she'll soon sort that out. But first she'll tell Adam she thinks they should cool it for a while. She slumps on to a bench. She hears footsteps running towards her. For a moment she thinks it's Adam. Then she quickly realises it's someone jogging. She feels a rush of disappointment.

When Adam walked off, was he really cross with her? She wouldn't be surprised. She's been awful company today. Adam, Adam, Adam, nothing can stop that name hammering away in her skull. He's given her more happiness than anyone else and a stronger helping of misery too. No, that's not fair. Yes, it is.

She holds her head in her hands. For one mad moment she had wanted to rip Adam out of her life. She thought she could do it, too. Now she can't think of anyone she'd rather see. And she badly wants to tell him about their baby.

She walks for miles, then she finally trudges home. Her mother is away in London meeting her editor and the house feels drab and still. She switches the television on and then she notices the red light on the answerphone is flashing dementedly. Surely it can't be Adam already. His lesson will only have finished ten minutes ago.

Her hand is shaking as she winds the message

15

back. Oh, don't let it be one of her mum's boring friends. Please God. There's a moment's silence and then Adam's voice. 'I am sincerely sorry I upset you. You were right to be annoyed,' (pause). 'I went to my lesson like you wanted. That's all really, except I love you and always will. Bye.'

And even before the message is finished, Becky is dialling his number. She has so much to tell him.

2 A Trip to Downing Street and Shock News

'You think I'm awful, don't you?' says Lauren.

'No,' says Cathy.

'So why are you looking all funny?'

'I always look like this.'

Lauren gazed down at her black mini-skirt. 'This is something I have to do. I need to feel I'm free, even if I'm not.' She shakes her head. 'I don't understand myself either.' Her voice becomes business-like: 'I told Jason I'm getting the 6.30 train, just in case he decides to turn up at the station to wave me off. Afterwards I might tell him I went to the play with just one boy, but tonight, remember, I'm going with the drama group. Okay.'

Then Lauren's parents emerge, her dad waving the car keys. 'You ready, Lauren?' and without waiting for an answer, he disappears out of the front door. Lauren gives Cathy a quick wave and disappears too. Cathy turns to face Lauren's mum, who is looking rather preoccupied. Have Lauren's parents had an argument? Perhaps Cathy had better make herself scarce. She is going upstairs when Lauren's mother calls, 'Cathy, would you like to have a cup of tea with us in the sitting room?'

'Oh, yes, all right, thank you.'

Six o'clock. It seems an odd time to sit down and have a cup of tea. Especially as they normally eat about half-past six. Cathy waits on the settee, feeling uneasy, without knowing why.

Lauren's mother appears with the tray of tea. She and Cathy make polite conversation until Lauren's dad returns and sits down heavily in his chair. Then, Lauren's mother says, 'Cathy, your mother came round this afternoon and we had a very long chat.'

'Oh, yes,' her voice is blurred and throaty.

'She left behind a wedding invitation for us, which we were very pleased to receive and she has one for you, too, which she'd obviously like to give you personally. So she was hoping you'd pop round and see her and Giles . . .'

'No, no, I can't.'

'This time, Cathy, I think you must.' Lauren's mother's tone is still soft but there's a firmness now, too. 'Cathy, we know it's hard but you've got to accept things now, come to terms with them.' Cathy raises her hand to her face. But this isn't

18

the way it was supposed to happen. No, the real ending was Cathy's mum rushing up to Cathy and saying, 'You were right. Giles is vile. Thank you, Cathy, for telling me. Now we can go back to how we were before.'

Oh, yes, please Mum, let's go back. Imagine you never met Giles. PLEASE. We were so happy then, just you, me and little Katie. We missed Dad deeply, of course, but we had each other and that was enough for me. Why wasn't it enough for you?

Go on, marry him, but you'll never see me again. Not that you'll care. For you chose him over me anyway. All at once Cathy lets out this tearing sob as a gust of misery takes hold of her. A handkerchief is thrust into Cathy's face and Lauren's dad looms over her.

'I'm sorry,' whispers Cathy.

'No, don't be sorry,' he cries. 'No need to stand on ceremony here, don't you worry about that.' He thumps back in his seat. 'Cathy, your mother is expecting you – and so are Giles and Katie, of course.'

Cathy tries to nod her head but suddenly it's made of lead. Then Lauren's dad says, 'Just remember Cathy, everyone has a right to their own life . . . even your mother.'

Cathy slowly gets up. She hasn't a clue what she's going to do. She knows what she wants to do: flounce in there and tear that stupid wedding

19

invitation up in their faces and then say, 'Giles, I wouldn't spit on you if you were on fire. And this is the last time I'll ever set foot in this house. I never want to see you again . . .' Tears start welling once more as Cathy shakes her head. 'I'll drive over then,' she says.

'No, you're far too upset to drive,' Lauren's mother says. She turns to her husband. 'You'll drive Cathy, won't you?'

'But I'm not staying long,' says Cathy, firmly. 'Just five minutes.'

Cathy is about to ring the doorbell but then she roots the key out of her bag. This is still her home after all. Her mum rushes towards her, then hesitates. She's smiling but her shoulders are hunched anxiously. Cathy feels a sudden pang of longing for her and then they're both hugging each other until her mum cries, 'I don't know why we're staying out in the hall. Come into the sitting room.'

Cathy follows her mum into the sitting room. Katie is immediately springing around her, while Scampi barks excitedly.

'Scampi, be quiet, there's a good boy . . . he's just so pleased to see you,' says her mother. 'Well, we all are.' And now, Giles has got up from the settee and is circling around them. If he makes a comment about Cathy's hair she's walking out. But he doesn't. Instead, he says, 'I'm really pleased about this,' extending his flabby hand. Cathy puts on her blank face and is sorely tempted to ignore the hand. But she can sense her mother just willing her to make a gesture. So she and Giles exchange limp handshakes.

He's clearly chuffed to bits now and is grinning all over his silly face. Look at him, thinks Cathy, with his tight jeans, sideburns and fake tan. He's nothing but, what's Lauren's phrase, a last-chance trendy. She can see him at the wedding reception, flirting round all the bridesmaids and being the last one to leave the dance floor. And yet, there's her mum, just oozing happiness.

'Cup of tea?' asks her mum.

'I can't stay long,' says Cathy. Lauren's dad promised he'd be back for her in half-an-hour.

'You've got time for a quick cuppa,' says Giles heartily. 'Want to help me, Katie?'

'Oh, yes.' Katie immediately bounds over to him and takes his hand.

After they've gone, Cathy's mum says, 'Sit down, sit down.'

Cathy perches on the settee, on which she notices a pile of family albums. Cathy used to love leafing through these, seeing the snaps of her parents when they were her age.

'Giles left one photo out for you to see.'

'I've seen them all, hundreds of times before,' snaps Cathy.

'Yes, but there was a picture here of me which he said reminded him of you.'

'Really.'

'Here we are.'

Cathy can feel her face freezing up again. She recognises the photo at once. There's her mum, about sixteen or seventeen, her chin resting on her hand, while smiling into the camera. And the picture's a riot. Her mum's hair is permed to death and she's got about fourteen rings on her fingers. Yet it always makes Cathy feel sad, too. For her mum's skin is perfect here and she looks so care-free and her eyes ... There's something about those eyes that does remind Cathy of that face she sneaks glances at in the morning. Funny, Cathy's never noticed it before. But now, the more she looks at the photograph, why, it's uncanny, the resemblance. Any second now the photograph will melt away totally, leaving just Cathy's features there.

She turns away from the photo and gazes across at her mother, to see the same eyes, looking so concerned. 'Yes, I can see the resemblance,' she mutters.

Then, Giles enters with a tea-tray and Katie is laughing and pointing to Giles's head, on which he is now sporting a blue tea-cosy. He slams the tray down in front of Cathy, then capers around the room, while Cathy's mum laughs indulgently and says, 'Take it off, Giles. What does he look like?' and Katie cries, 'I dared him to do it.'

Cathy averts her gaze to the pot of tea. She'll have to force down half a cup. Then she sights a white envelope propped up against the sugar bowl. And suddenly, everyone is watching her again. She knows instantly what it is, of course. But even so, the first words punch her eyes so hard, they start blinking furiously:

The honour of *Cathy Adams's* presence
is requested at the marriage of
Mrs Robert Adams
and
Mr Giles Shaw

Cathy looks away and takes a gulp of tea. It's far too strong, or, as her dad would say, 'You could stand a spoon up in it.' Her dad! This is all his fault, dying like that. Then she sees her mum looking at her, just begging her to say something positive.

'I'll be there,' says Cathy huskily and takes another mouthful of tea. Giles and Kate chorus their agreement. 'When we're away in Venice,' her mum can't help giving a little tremor of pleasure as she says this, 'we'll need someone to look after Katie.'

'Yes, yes, okay,' cries Cathy. They're rushing

her now, pushing her faster than she wants to go. And how cramped and tiny this sitting room feels. Can she bear to be cooped up here again with Giles, night after night? Then, to her great relief, she hears a car purr into the drive.

'That'll be Mr Davies,' she says. She leaps up and so does everyone else. There are more handshakes and then, as her mum hugs her goodbye, Cathy thinks, everyone's being nice to me, but I'm just being a good loser, aren't I? Giles has won. She knows she shouldn't think of it like that. She knows Lauren's dad is right, you can't deny someone their own life, not even your mum. But it's hard and even though she's smiling bravely at them all clustered round the doorway, Cathy feels so hollow inside. If only Jez were here. He'd somehow make all this seem absurdly funny.

Outside, she takes in the fact that its not Lauren's dad waiting for her in the drive. It's . . . Her heart turns a somersault and Jason bounds out of the car. 'Taxi, ma'am.'

'What are you doing here?' she cries, scrambling inside.

Jason grins across at her. 'I just knew you'd want a lift. Having an especially brilliant brain, I picked up your . . .'

'You went round to Lauren's house and her mum and dad told you, didn't they?'

Jason answers this with another question. 'So what's the crack in there?'

'Nothing much. My mum is getting married to Giles in a few weeks. Today, they gave me the wedding invite, which I'm so thrilled about.'

Jason doesn't say anything for a minute, then he asks, 'Is your mum happy about it?'

'Oh yes, she is now.'

'I'd just let her get on with it, then.'

'That's all I can do. If I force my mum to choose, I'll lose, won't I? So I'm going back. I can't go on staying at Lauren's. They've been so nice, but I agreed I'd look after Katie when mum and Giles are away on their honeymoon.' She shudders.

'But you won't be living at home for ever, will you?'

'No, that's true,' says Cathy.

'And anyway,' he goes on, 'I think families are over-rated. They're nice in their way, but optional.'

Cathy smiles to herself. How can families be optional? But she likes to hear Jason talk. 'How do you mean?' she asks.

'Okay,' he says. 'Take me. I'm not that close to my parents. We don't even talk most of the time. We haven't for years, not since my Dad ran off with a woman.'

'You never mentioned that,' says Cathy.

'Haven't I?' says Jason, vaguely. 'He came back but I can't handle that crap. My point is, though,

25

I'm managing perfectly okay without them. In fact, I don't need them at all now. See?'

'Yes,' says Cathy, softly, 'I see.' She peers out of the window. 'By the way, where are we going?'

'Nowhere. I just thought you'd want me to drive you around for a while.'

'That's very thoughtful of you,' says Cathy.

'I know. Do you fancy going somewhere then?'

She sits up. 'Yes. Where?'

'Downing Street?'

She stares at him in surprise. 'What, now?'

'Yeah, you see it so often on the news, I thought it'd be cool to check it out . . .'

'But it's miles away.'

'So what. Do you want to see Downing Street?'

She smiles. 'Yes I do. Very much.'

Cathy sails through the front door. Then she hears, 'And where have you been?' Lauren is pulling her into the kitchen. 'I thought I was the dirty stop-out tonight.'

'Jason took me for a drive,' says Cathy.

'I know, Dad told me . . . he also told me about you going round to your mum's. Was it awful?'

'Yeah, but still,' Cathy shrugs her shoulders. 'Forget that now.'

Lauren gets the message. 'Coffee?' she asks.

'I'd love one.'

Lauren switches the kettle on. 'So where did you go for your drive?'

'Downing Street.'

Lauren whirls round. 'All that way. No wonder you've been gone so long.'

'It was Jason's idea. He just said, "Fancy going to Downing Street?" '

Lauren sits down again. 'And what was it like?'

Cathy leans forward. 'Oh, Lauren, it was fascinating. First of all we saw the Thames and Jason was convinced he saw this body or a part of one in there; we were looking at the river for ages. Then we walked to Downing Street, which is such a funny street, and there were two policemen outside; one was in a little police box having a cuppa, and there was this police van circling round, too. The moon was full, which made it all seem so unreal, like a film set. You expected someone to come along and wheel it away any minute.'

Lauren gets up to make the coffee and when she sits down again, Cathy continues, without any prompting. 'And then, Lauren, this guy in a fisherman's jersey, really weird-looking, started following us. Jason reckoned he was either a drug dealer or an under-cover cop. We didn't hang around to find out, but it was all so intriguing. And then on the way back I just yarned on about my mum and Giles and Jason was just so – well, you know how he really listens.'

Lauren says, 'Yes, Jason is good when you're feeling down. I'm sorry I wasn't here. My dad wondered if he should have told me ... '

'Oh no, no,' says Cathy. 'No sense in spoiling your night. By the way, how was the play? I'm sorry, I should have asked you that ages ago.'

'It was brilliant, actually, and there was a really good atmosphere.'

'And did Russell behave himself?'

'Oh, yes,' Lauren laughs her throaty laugh. 'It's funny. Jason would have hated tonight, he really would. Yet, I couldn't help wishing he was there. I missed him, isn't that silly?'

'No, I can understand that,' says Cathy softly.

'Still, I'm glad he was there for you.'

'He said he'll even go to the wedding with me too – provided there's free beer all night.'

Lauren laughs. 'Isn't that typical of him? You know, he sends me crazy sometimes but when he's not there ... Did he say anything about me tonight?'

'A bit.'

'Tell me, tell me.'

'He just said how wonderful you were and how bad he felt about that night.'

'So he should ... Still, I've finally forgiven him. Oh yes, I know what I meant to tell you. On the pad, there's a message from Becky. She wants us all to meet up for a drink tomorrow night. Do you know anything about this?'

'No, and I saw her today, too.'

'I thought it was a bit sudden. I wonder what it's all about?'

Jason hauls the leather chair over to where the other five are sitting.

'Happy now?' asks Lauren.

'Yeah,' Jason sinks into the chair. 'These chairs are wicked. I'll have three or four in my house, probably in the hall.'

'You know who you look like?' says Mark. 'Don Corleoni, in *The Godfather*.'

Jason starts waving his hands and, in a heavy Italian accent, says, 'So Adam and Becky, why have you called us here and how can the Godfather help you?'

Adam grins nervously. 'I'm going to buy you all some drinks first.' They are sitting in The White Hart, picked by Adam and Becky because, 'they wanted to talk'. Behind them is a bookcase and a display of plates with fruit on them, while horse brasses trail down the other walls.

'No, we can't wait another second,' says Lauren. 'Tell us now.'

'Yes, come on,' says Cathy. 'What is the big mystery?'

Adam looks at Becky. 'No mystery ... it's

29

just . . .' He really wants to tell them the good news, but yet he doesn't. He twists his face into a grin. 'Distinguished friends,' he says. He hopes his voice sounds light and relaxed, just like Jason's does at moments like this. 'Becky and I wanted you to be the very first to know, we're getting engaged. Although there are no rings to flash around yet, there will be. He turns to Becky and laughs nervously. 'They all look stunned.'

'It's a bit drastic, isn't it?' says Jason.

'Congratulations, anyway,' says Cathy. 'It's just a bit of a shock.' Then she looks at Lauren, whose eyes seem to be growing larger and larger. Neither she nor Mark say a word.

'And there's another bit of good news,' continues Adam, more than a bit desperately. He lowers his voice to a confiding whisper, 'Becky's expecting our baby.' And before anyone can respond, Adam announces, 'And now I'm going to buy you all a drink to celebrate our good news. All have your usual, will you?' Everyone just gapes at him. 'Okay, won't be long.'

Then Jason says, 'I'll give you a hand, mate,' and disappears with him.

'Someone say something,' whispers Becky.

'Congratulations,' says Cathy. 'Definitely, congratulations.' She turns to Mark. 'Did you know about this?'

Mark puts down his pint glass. He's been drinking steadily throughout the evening. 'Some, not all. I didn't know about the engagement.'

'No, it was very sudden,' says Becky. 'We just happened to go into the jeweller's yesterday and Adam asked me if I'd like to try on some engagement rings.' She gives a little shiver of pleasure. 'We couldn't afford any of them, of course, except for this fake diamond ring which neither of us wanted, but the girl behind the counter didn't seem to mind. In fact, I think she was quite bored, as she showed us her engagement ring, which had this huge diamond, but neither Adam nor I liked it very much, because the ring itself looked . . .'

'So what did Adam say about the baby?' cuts in Lauren.

'He's very happy about it.'

Lauren raises an eyebrow.

'And so am I.'

'You're going to keep it, then,' continues Lauren.

'Oh, yes, definitely.'

'How many weeks are you?'

'Eight weeks.'

Lauren suddenly hisses, 'Then get rid of it.'

Becky looks shocked. 'But I couldn't, not now.'

'It's just an egg,' snaps Lauren. 'You eat eggs for breakfast.' Her voice softens. 'Look Becky, one day when you're settled, have six kids if you like, but not now. Do you realise what you're doing,

31

you're giving up twenty years of your life and you haven't started to live yet. I'm sorry, but I don't think you and Adam have thought this out at all.' She turns to Cathy and Mark, 'Have they?'

Mark shrugs his shoulders. 'Nothing to do with me,' he mutters.

Cathy says, gently, 'Perhaps you and Adam do need to talk about this a bit more. Have you told your mum yet?'

'Here we go, drinks all round.' Adam squeezes into his place again and quickly takes in the tense, tight smiles. Then he looks again at Becky. She looks pale and anxious. His friends have really let him down tonight, just when he and Becky really needed some support.

He puts his arm around Becky, then says, 'Our good news seems to have gone down like a glass of beer with a nail in it, doesn't it?' He gives a dry laugh. 'I just want you all to know, that Becky and I are really happy about this. We'd hoped you would be too. We'd hoped also, one of you might even have proposed a toast to us. But not to worry, I'll do it now: raise your glasses please, to Adam and Becky.'

'And when Adam made that toast, he looked so hurt, I felt awful,' says Cathy. 'And the way he and Becky walked out . . . They didn't even say, goodbye, did they?'

'It was such an awful atmosphere,' sighs Lauren, 'and I hate atmospheres.' She turns to Mark. 'How are you feeling?'

'All right,' he mutters. Lauren, Cathy, Mark and Jason are sitting in Lauren's kitchen, conducting a post-mortem on the events earlier in the evening.

Lauren says, 'I suppose I was a bit blunt. I could have been gentler.'

'It was a shock, though,' says Cathy.

'That's it,' cries Lauren. 'I mean, when they said they had news, it did cross my mind that they were engaged, but then I thought, why get engaged now? I did come on a bit strong, didn't I? I just felt it had to be said, after all they could sacrifice their whole life. I wanted to snap them out of it, make them see . . . Oh, I don't know.'

'Her mum will sort it out,' says Cathy. 'She's really nice.'

Mark stands up.

'Are you feeling sick?' asks Lauren, at once.

'No, just want another glass of water, that's all,' says Mark.

'If you do feel sick, you will run out right away, won't you?' asks Lauren.

'Yes,' says Mark, sitting down again with a glass of water.

'You're very quiet,' says Cathy, turning to Jason.

'I hate babies,' declares Jason. 'And women who have them turn into really annoying people. They

33

wear dungarees and are always kicking their prams against your legs down the market.'

'Wow, that's really helpful,' says Lauren, with heavy sarcasm. But Cathy remembers that day in social education, when they all had to watch a film about birth and Jason turned quite green and declared, 'This is gross.'

Lauren presses on. 'So you've no advice for Becky and Adam?'

Cathy sees Jason shift uneasily. In a crisis, Jason's the one you turn to first. How many problems has he solved for them over the years? But in this instance, she suspects, he's totally lost. Finally, he says, 'The way I see it, Adam and Becky have got two choices. On the one hand they can slip into the rented television life; you know, living in a bedsit, having children and grandchildren and generally, be banal. Or they could do something different . . .' Everyone's staring at him intently. 'They could run off and be cavemen.'

'Cavemen,' echo Lauren and Cathy.

'Yes, that's right,' says Jason. 'They can live in a cave and eat berries.' Then, seeing their faces, he says, 'Or they could have a hippy child and go and live in a commune. That's an alternative.'

'No, it's not,' says Lauren. 'For a start, what are they going to live on?'

'Ah, you don't need half the crap people spend on babies these days. Think about it. What do you

34

actually need? Nappies and food, that's all. But most parents are off buying mini-golf-clubs and beds on hire-purchase.'

'So they don't need beds, do they?' asks Lauren, half-smiling. 'Where are they going to sleep then?'

'In the caves,' says Jason. Then suddenly, his face breaks into a smile. 'I don't know what the hell I'm talking about,' he says and starts to laugh.

Cathy suspects that he's laughing to cover up his embarrassment, but it's so infectious that she and Lauren join in too. It's actually a relief to laugh, after all the heaviness tonight.

Mark gets to his feet. 'I'm going home,' he announces. 'See you.' He stumbles to the kitchen door.

'I'll come with you, mate,' says Jason. He turns to Lauren and Cathy. 'I'm going to see him home.'

Lauren nods in agreement. 'Mark's been strange all evening. I think he needs someone now.'

Mark staggers in from the garden shaking his head at Jason. 'No, I still feel as if I'm going to be sick, but in the next half-hour.' He closes the back door quietly behind him. The last thing he wants now is one of his parents wandering downstairs and seeing him like this.

Jason is standing by the window, drinking a mug of coffee. 'Coffee?'

Mark shudders. 'No, nothing.' He sinks on to a chair by the kitchen table.

Jason grins. 'Whenever you're drunk, your face inflates like a chipmunk. And tonight, you're out of your skull, aren't you?'

Mark groans. 'Switch the light off, will you?'

Jason switches the light off, then sits down opposite Mark. There's an easy, companionable silence until Mark asks, 'Is it my imagination, or is the ceiling sliding down on to the floor?'

'I'm afraid, mate, you've got the spins. Do you want me to put the light back on?'

'No, no,' says Mark hastily. 'No lights.' Then he says, 'I persuaded Becky to go to the clinic, you know, and I went with her, held her hand. She wouldn't have gone if it hadn't been for me.'

'Good old Mark,' says Jason gently.

'Yeah, good old Mark,' repeats Mark angrily. 'Everyone's friend but that's as far as it goes. She never breathed a word to me about the engagement, though. She doesn't need me now, you see. She's got Adam. So I'm just a cast-off again. He'll be having all the glory, presents, cards, telling everyone, "Yes, Becky is my fiancée." He's wearing the jewellery, but who has to polish it when it gets scratched? ME! No, he's got everything he wants and it's not sodding fair.' Mark's voice is getting louder. He stops for a moment, then carries on in a sort of screaming whisper, 'I put them together, you know. And I really wish I hadn't, because I've got so much more to offer than Adam. I've got a better brain, and I'm going further. I'll be on the student executive soon. I bet I get better A level grades than Adam,' he pauses again. 'Anyway, he doesn't appreciate Becky, not how I appreciate her. No, the only thing Adam's got is a motorbike. He hasn't got a personality. And everyone thinks he's so deep.' He lets out a strange, choking laugh. 'If I'd wanted to, I could have taken Becky away from him. She liked me too, you know. That first day, she could have been mine, if I hadn't taken her into the hall. And I could have broken them up. I know what traps to set.' He lets out another choking sob, 'Why the hell didn't I?'

Jason, who hasn't tried to interrupt Mark once, says slowly, 'Because you've got principles.'

'Principles.' Mark spits the word back at him. 'What use are they?'

Jason replies. 'If you haven't got any principles, you're not a real person, are you, you're just a shell. You're nothing.'

Mark doesn't say anything for a moment, then mutters, 'I'm a mug.'

'Yeah – and you're a sound geezer,' replies Jason. 'I'd be proud to shake you by the hand.' In the darkness, he stretches out his hand to Mark. Mark takes hold of it and then totters to his feet.

He says, 'When I was doing the Karaoke at The

White Hart, I felt like I owned the world, you know. Now they want me to stand for the Student Union and I'll do that too. I'm going to do so many things, Jason.' He puts his hand over his mouth: 'Now, I'm going to be sick,' and rushed out to the garden.

'I suppose we ought to go back,' says Adam.

'Yes, we ought,' murmurs Becky. But neither of them moves. Becky wishes you could climb into moments like this, pulling yourself deeper and deeper inside, until you never had to return to the pale, dim light of reality.

But in the end, it is Adam who drags her away. 'Do you think you will tell your mum tomorrow?'

She senses he wants her to. He's feeling let down by everyone tonight, and on his own. He wants someone else to share the responsibility. Becky does, too. It's just she knows her mum will be so disappointed and blame herself.

'Yes, I'll tell her tomorrow,' she says.

'I may as well tell my mum too,' he says. 'Get it all over with.' Then he takes her hand and kisses it. 'You should have a ring here,' he cries. 'And one day, you'll have a ring to knock everyone's eyes out.'

Becky shakes her head. 'It doesn't matter, it's not important. All that matters, is us.' She half-smiles. 'The three of us.'

3 *Mark's Brilliant Plan*

Becky presses her face against the glass. A thick, grey mist is taking hold of Cartford. The houses opposite are sinking fast, and the dark shapes passing the window seem eerily unreal. Becky frowns with concentration. If she looks a bit harder, will her mum appear? Where is she?

She and Adam had made a pact, that they would tell their parents (or their mothers, anyway) about the baby at exactly the same time: half-past two this afternoon. They felt it might bring them luck.

But now, it's nearly four o'clock and Becky's getting so wound up. Perhaps she should go to the loo. People always turn up when you're in the loo, don't they? Instead, she glares at the television. She'd switched it on to relax her, but now she finds it annoying.

It's almost five o'clock when her mum finally

waltzes in. By now, Becky is so tense her voice seems to have gone into spasm. 'Where have you been?' she croaks.

'My friend, Paula, had to take her cat to the vet's for a one-way trip. And to make it worse, it wasn't a very pleasant cat. Still, Paula felt she had to be there when the deed was done and I went along for moral support. Or was I just playing truant from my writing, because the new chapter's not going at all well? I need an injection of caffeine, yes, that is a hint.'

When Becky returns with the coffee, her mum is sprawled across the couch, gazing at an old black-and-white film on television. 'That's Vincent Price, can you believe he ever looked that young? I think he's playing the callow hero.'

'Mum, would you mind if I switched the television off . . . I've got some news for you.'

'Good news?'

'Sort of, I think so.' Becky clicks off the television and falls into a chair, opposite her mum. Now the moment is finally here, she doesn't want to say it. Yet, she'll explode if she doesn't. She looks at her mum quickly then turns away again. 'Actually, I think I'm pregnant.'

'Think,' her mum repeats the word as if she's never heard it before.

'I know I am.' Becky wants to do something with her hands now, like pick her coffee cup up, only she daren't as they're shaking so much. She darts another glance at her mother. She's sitting up straight, as she asks, 'How many weeks?'

'Nine.'

'It's Adam's?'

'Yes.' Becky whispers the last word. She suddenly feels deeply embarrassed and prays her mum won't ask her any more about that. She knows she's let her mum down. There's no need to rub her nose in it.

'What do you and Adam want to do?'

'We want to keep it.'

Her mum doesn't reply to this, just looks as if she's stopped breathing. Becky blurts out, 'You're disappointed in me, aren't you?'

'No, no. Only, you haven't given yourself a chance, have you?' There's a definite throb of anger in her mum's voice now. 'You've not had a chance to find out anything yet, have you? You realise your life is going to be turned upside down, don't you?'

'Mum, don't.' whispers Becky. 'Don't be against us.'

Her mum gives her a hard stare, gets up, hovering awkwardly for a moment, before half-kneeling by her chair. She says, 'Becky, I was twenty-two when I had you and I felt that was too young to be a mother. Of course, I was a total idiot.' Becky smiles. 'And I hadn't anything to draw on. I had

41

to do my growing up alongside you. I always hoped you'd have a better chance.'

'But Adam and I will really love our baby.'

'I know you will,' says her mum. 'It's just,' she sighs, 'I can't tell you how much a baby changes you. You're an instant grown-up. For a start, you're going to have to stretch yourself in so many ways, you know.'

'I know,' murmurs Becky, but even as she's saying this a little voice inside her is saying, do you really know what you're taking on? Can you really cope?

'And Becky, everything changes. Everything. Even little things. You don't even sleep in the way you did. Once you have children, that old deep sleep is gone forever. For then, it's as if you develop antennae and the child's slightest sound, tiniest whimper, will waken you . . .' Becky's mum is talking to Becky as if she's an equal. Becky wants this, only it's chilling too. It's as if, right now, Becky is turning into her mum and she's not ready for that yet. Is she? Suddenly, she's all confused.

The doorbell rings. Her mum swears under her breath. 'I'll get rid of whoever . . .'

Seconds later her mum reappears and Becky lets out a low gasp. 'Hello, Mrs Rosen,' she says. They exchange tense, social smiles. Mrs Rosen looks cold and uncomfortable.

'Let me take your coat for you,' says Becky's mum.

'No, that's all right. I can't stay long anyway. I just wanted a word.' Then there's silence, which positively shrieks, 'Get lost, Becky.' Becky gets up very slowly. Really, she should stay. After all, she's the one who's going to have a baby. But instead, she'll go outside and eavesdrop. 'I'll get myself a drink. Would anyone . . .' There's a chorus of, 'No, thank you.'

In the kitchen, Becky stares out of the window. She can't see anything now. Everything's been swallowed up. The mist has taken it all over. That's how she feels, taken over. Her old life has been wiped out, leaving what – what can she see ahead for her? Her mum's right. Her life's never going to be the same again. Yesterday she was excited about it all: now, she just feels frightened.

She gets up and tiptoes back to the lounge. The first voice she hears is Mrs Rosen's. 'This is Adam's fault. I blame him for this. And I know his father will too. He took advantage of Becky. I told him that today.' Poor Adam, thinks Becky. How she longs to talk to him.

Then she hears her mum say, 'They both acted irresponsibly, now they've got to act responsibly. Whatever decision they take isn't going to be easy.'

'But Becky cannot keep it,' cries Mrs Rosen. 'If she does, it will only drag them both down. And then there's the whole problem of who is going to look after it. Not to mention the money. With them both at college, where's that coming from? I don't suppose Becky's father . . .'

'No,' says Becky's mum flatly. 'No help there.' Too right, thinks Becky. Her dad's so tight he squeaks.

'So we're in agreement then,' says Adam's mother. 'They must get rid of it.' Becky's hand strains forward. She should burst in. How dare that woman start laying down the law about what she and Adam should and shouldn't do? How dare she?

Mrs Rosen continues. 'And then Adam's ambitious. I'm sure Becky is too. We can't let them throw their futures away like this.'

'All we can do is talk through the options for them. We can't decide for them. It has to be their decision. We just have to help them come to grips with what's happened . . .' Becky's mum is talking sense yet her voice seems to rise from a deep well of sadness. And even standing outside, Becky can pick up her disappointment.

But it is going to be all right, isn't it? Who can reassure her? No one. Because no one thinks she should keep the baby. No one, except Adam. All at once, Becky rushes out into the mist.

Lauren's father hauls the bag into the car, then

turns to Cathy and gives a slight bow. 'Your bags ma'am, safely delivered and I won't even ask for a tip.'

Cathy gazes around at the three people clustered around her car. She says thickly, 'You've all made me so welcome.'

'It's been a pleasure, you've been the ideal guest,' says Lauren's mum. Lauren's dad sweeps Cathy up into his arms and gives her one of his bear-hugs. 'You're going to be all right,' he says. Then he stomps away. Mrs Davies kisses Cathy on both cheeks, murmurs, 'Go carefully in this mist,' and follows him.

Cathy smiles after them, then says to Lauren, 'Aren't your parents brilliant?'

'They have their moments.'

'And to think I used to be really scared of your dad.'

'He's a pussy cat really. But I'm going to miss you. What about all our little gossips at night?'

'I know,' says Cathy softly.

'Don't go, then.'

'Lauren, if I don't leave now I'll never go. I know it.'

'That's all right. Never leave – I'd love that. We'll go on together, just you and me.'

'Until you get married.'

'No, my husband can live next door, or in a separate wing, or something. So, don't go.'

Cathy hesitates. 'No, I'd better go back. Mum's been on at me to come home, long before this. The wedding's only two weeks away, you know.' Her voice tightens. 'I'm only going four roads away. I can pop over in five minutes, two if I drive.'

'But it's not the same,' says Lauren, with a little pout. She's gone all girlish. 'I really, really, don't want you to go.'

'I don't want to go either,' Cathy's voice tightens again. 'I'm dreading it, to tell the truth. Everyone is trying so hard. Giles is smiling at me from every doorway, asking me about college, trying to take an interest. But it is my home and I miss my mum. And Scampi.'

'Oh, well, clear off then,' says Lauren.

Cathy laughs. 'See you tomorrow.' Then she gets into the car. 'Is Jason coming round tonight?'

'Probably.'

'Say hello, from me.' The smile slips off her face. 'I can't tell you how much I'm dreading this.'

Lauren waves Cathy off, then walks back into the house, feeling distinctly lost. Having Cathy stay had been like having a sister. It quite shocked her how much she'd liked that.

'I'm going to miss her,' she announces to her parents in the lounge. Her mum is watering the plants. Her father is wearing the thickest glasses imaginable which make him look about ten years older, and rustling *The Times* in a way that always indicates he's annoyed about something.

'We will all miss her,' says her mum. 'She hasn't got a bad thought in her head, that girl. We've always liked Cathy.' Her tone changes. 'I suppose you'll be spending even more time with Jason, now.'

'Not necessarily.'

Her father looks up. 'Oh yes, you will,' he booms. 'As it is, the two of you can't exist apart from each other for more than a few hours. Well, you can say goodbye to any chance of passing A levels now.'

Lauren gapes at him. 'What do you mean?'

'Your mother and I know exactly what's going on,' says her father. 'Since you've taken up with him, you've stopped working.'

'No, I haven't,' cries Lauren.

'You're not working as you used to, are you Lauren? You can't deny that,' says her mother.

No, Lauren can't deny that. And although she'd never admit it, Jason is partly (if not mainly) to blame. Although she'll tell him she's working, he still turns up at the same time, saying, 'Come on, leave your books. Do that another time,' and he makes studying seem so boffish and boring. So Lauren has been leaving her books. Yet she's felt cross with Jason for not understanding she needs

47

to work sometimes and cross with herself for being so weak-willed.

'Yes, I am working,' cries Lauren. 'Honestly.'

Her dad flings his paper down, sweat glistening on his brow. 'We don't know if it's worth you staying at college. You're not going to pass any exams.'

'Oh, thanks a lot,' exclaims Lauren.

'You may as well leave college now and go and work in the supermarket. Like him.'

'Dad, Jason doesn't work in a supermarket, he works in the sports shop.'

Her dad shakes his head. 'He's still a shop assistant.'

'Oh, you snob,' cries Lauren. 'You've really got your knife into poor Jason, haven't you? Just because he stands up to you.' She turns to her mum. 'I thought you liked Jason.'

'I do,' says her mum. 'And if he's happy doing shop-work, that's fine but that's not what you want, is it? You're academic. He's not. Don't let him throw your talent away, that's all we're saying.'

'He's not going to do that,' says Lauren. 'He wants me to do well,' she adds, not completely convincingly.

Her dad raises his hand as if he's umpiring a football match. 'We are very concerned about this, but we'll leave it,' he pauses, then adds ominously, 'for now.'

*

48

Dare Mark take one more look? Mark dares. He walks back to the noticeboard outside the refectory – and that list headed STUDENT EXECUT-IVES. Beside *Entertainments*, is that name of names: MARK APPLETON. Every time he sees that, Mark gets this rush of energy, this feeling that he can do anything.

Yesterday at the student executive meeting he had lots of ideas, all of which everyone seemed to agree with. He's been on a crest of a wave ever since.

Then, there's this heavy tap on his shoulder and he sees Adam grinning shyly at him. Adam points to Mark's name on the list. 'I know that guy. You've done all right, haven't you?'

'Cheers. We had a meeting yesterday and all ended up down the pub. But I'm organising more discos, more trips . . .' Mark rattles on, while inside he's squirming with embarrassment and shame. He still can't believe the way he slagged Adam off that night. It was so lucky, only Jason heard it. The day after, Mark saw Jason and said, 'I had a bit of a tantrum last night, didn't I? Jason replied, 'Don't worry about it. You had to get it off your chest.'

But a week later, Mark still feels guilty about his outburst. He and Adam go back a long way. Even when he was mad, he had no business saying things like, 'Adam hasn't got a personality'. That was just pure spite. For Mark's always rather envied Adam's style, especially the way he never pushes himself forward and yet people notice him anyway.

'Shall we sit down for a minute,' says Adam.

'Yeah, sure,' says Mark.

Most students are going back to lessons now, save for a large group huddled around a card game. Adam walks right down the refectory and picks a table in the corner.

'Actually,' says Adam, 'I'm on the run.'

'Who from?'

'Robocop, alias Garnett, my personal tutor.'

'Don't think I know him.'

'You're lucky. You can't miss him: big bulging eyes, no chin and breath that reeks of vegetable soup.'

'He sounds excellent. So why's he after you?'

'The usual stuff. I've been missing lessons again, so it's his job to give me grief. He's out searching for me now. Only this time, I reckon he's going to chuck me out.'

'Nah, they have to give you warnings.'

'I've had them,' says Adam, matter of factly.

'They won't chuck you out,' says Mark.

'That's what Becky says. She also says, she hardly sees you, these days.'

Mark starts guiltily. In fact, he's only spoken to Becky once since that night in The White Hart. The following day she came round to his house and said she and Adam had meant to tell him about

50

the engagement first but they'd run out of time. He still thought that was a bit feeble, to tell the truth. No, as soon as Adam came on the scene, Mark was just forgotten and had to find things out with everyone else.

But all that seems trivial now, compared with what's facing Adam and Becky.

'How are things?' asks Mark.

'Okayish. We told our parents last week. Things got a bit hairy.' Adam smiles to himself; that's the understatement of the year. His mum freaked out when he told her, totally freaked. Then she stormed off to see Becky's mum and Becky turned up at his house. She was shaking. Adam tried to calm her down, reassure her, yet, all the time he had this hollow feeling in his stomach. Then the hollow feeling somehow oozed up his neck, until finally he could taste it. Yet, all the time, he was saying, 'It's going to be all right. We're going to be okay.'

Since then, well, some days it's all right, other days the responsibility of it all pulls him down. But he can't think about anything else. Becky's his whole life now.

'No wonder you've been dropping out of college,' says Mark. 'Who wouldn't?'

Adam gives a short laugh. 'Yeah, it's a good excuse to skive, isn't it?'

'If you need any help with anything . . . '

'Thanks, mate. I appreciate that. Oh, hell.'

'What?'

'Robocop's just seen me and he's got steam coming out of his ears.' He gets up. 'I think it's execution time.'

'They won't chuck you out,' says Mark.

Adam grins faintly and pats Mark on the shoulder.

After Adam's gone, Mark suffers another outbreak of guilt, a bad attack this time. He hasn't been much of a friend to either Adam or Becky this last week, has he? He's abandoned them, because of his own little whinges. And Adam and Becky need their friends right now.

It's then he has an idea. He can see it already, almost to the last detail. Why, that's brilliant.

777. Adam turns the numbers on the combination lock, magic numbers even now, that's what they are. The secret code to a world no one outside the seven of them has ever entered, or ever will. Except, maybe, one day, he and Becky will take their son or daughter by the hand . . . He smiles at the idea. He turns to Becky, 'Mark should be here any second,' he says. Then he opens the hut door, sniffs in the familiar musty smell and lets out a low whistle of amazement. For a pink flashlight is beaming across at them lighting up six balloons swaying precariously from the ceiling, while on the

lino is a tray containing six wine glasses and two dishes of twiglets and crisps.

Then there's a flurry of footsteps and Jason, Cathy, Lauren and Mark burst in. Cathy and Lauren are carrying a cake with Adam and Becky's names in silver. Jason is brandishing a bottle and Mark, laughing nervously, lets off a party-popper, which flies into Becky's hair. 'Here, have one,' he says to Becky. 'And you, Adam.' He hands them round like cigars. 'Got twelve for 99p.'

'I don't know what to say,' cries Becky.

'Don't say anything,' replies Jason. 'Get drunk instead. This bottle looks like sparkling wine, doesn't it?'

'£3.99 from the Wine Rack,' interrupts Mark.

'But if you shake the wine hard it turns into champagne and the top will even fly out like so . . .' Seconds later 'champagne' is gushing everywhere, including into six wine glasses.

Mark says to Becky, 'I'm sorry the cake isn't very cute but this was a real rush job.' The party was Mark's idea. He said how they'd all let Adam and Becky down and a show of solidarity was needed, urgently. So then, he, Cathy and Lauren had raced around the town in about an hour, buying as much as they could afford.

'For your wedding we'll do something much more special,' says Cathy.

'Oh yeah, that will be the mother of all parties, this is just the second cousin,' says Mark.

Becky says, 'No, this is perfect, just the . . .'

'The inner circle,' prompts Jason. Becky nods. 'This has been an inner circle production,' says Jason.

'Mark, your toast,' prompts Lauren.

'It's okay, I hadn't forgotten.' Mark rubs his hands together. 'Adam and Becky, we want to say, congratulations on all your news and good luck.'

'We'll need it,' says Adam.

'No, you'll make it,' says Mark. 'You'll pull through this, and bring forth into the world a beautiful babe . . . and I'm going to be the godfather.'

'No way,' says Jason, mock-angrily. 'It's got to be me.'

'Come on, Jason,' replies Mark. 'I'll remember his birthdays more than you.'

'But I'll give it better presents,' says Jason.

'It!' cries Lauren.

'Well, all babies are "It" aren't they?' says Jason. Lauren groans.

'Just get on with the toast, Mark,' murmurs Cathy.

'Yes, right, that's it really, raise your glasses please, to Adam and Becky.'

'Adam and Becky,' is echoed and glasses are clinked loudly.

'So what are you going to call it?' asks Jason. 'If it's a boy, you can call it after me, if you like.'

Mark says, 'Just don't call it Rambo or Ebenezer or . . .'

'Or Jeremiah,' says Lauren.

'And actually, who are the godparents going to be?' asks Mark.

Godparents. That gives Adam a start. His immediate response is, we don't have them and what's the point of them anyway. For a moment, he feels oddly stranded. He hates the idea of god-parents, yet he can't begin to explain why. Besides, this isn't the moment to get heavy.

'I think we should all be godparents, Jez as well,' says Mark.

Adam recovers himself. 'Yeah, why not,' he says. Two balloons drop down off the ceiling on to the floor.

'I told you we needed more blu-tack,' says Mark. 'I wanted to get some helium balloons. Ever tried those, Becky?' She shakes her head. 'You suck it in and it makes you talk like a smurf. We often did it. Jason used to pretend it never worked on him.'

'Anyway,' says Adam, 'this is brilliant.'

'You haven't tasted the cake yet,' says Mark.

'And I really want to thank you,' continues Adam. 'Actually, we've got another bit of news for you, if you can take the excitement.'

All at once there's not even the whisper of a

sound. Slightly embarrassed, Adam says, 'It's nothing really, it's just I've packed up college. Robocop put me on report yesterday and said I'd be chucked out in two weeks if I didn't improve and I thought, do I need this hassle. NO. So today, I rang Becky, then I rang up my video shop and they've offered me a full-time post there from next Monday.'

'But won't you get bored with that?' asks Lauren.

'No more than I do at college,' says Adam. 'And at least I'll be earning money, which we need.' Lauren opens her mouth but then closes it again. She said too much last time.

'And now over to Becky,' says Adam, 'who – '

'Who has walked out of college too,' she says. 'I haven't been working, so I thought, why not. I'll pop in and see Mark and everyone. But I'll be at the *Pizza Paradiso*, full-time.' She takes Adam's hand. 'We want to prove that we can see this through without any help from anyone and that we're not playing at this. We're really going to look after our baby and right now, more than anything else, we need money. So if it means we have to give up college, that's what we'll have to do.'

'I don't think I could have done that,' says Cathy slowly. 'And I think that deserves another toast. Everyone, here's to Becky and Adam, who really do deserve every happiness.'

*

56

Afternoon lessons have finished and the college is deserted, save for a few students clustered around the entrance and Lauren, who is in the staffroom having a tutorial with her Communications teacher. Lauren needs this tutorial, as she is giving a talk in front of the whole group tomorrow and she still hasn't decided what she's going to talk about.

'So, Lauren, how about a talk in defence of advertising?'

'Yes, that sounds . . .' but Lauren's attention is distracted by the sight of Jason peering in through the staffroom window. What's he doing here? She hides a smile. For now, Jason is pressing his nose up against the glass, just as he did at school when he was sent out of class (which he was, frequently).

She tries to tune back into her tutor, Barry Edwards. He's got one of those unfortunate faces, which looks as if it has been put on a vice and squashed. Jason's pointing at his face and laughing. Lauren very nearly bursts out laughing too. Her lecturer is saying, 'As far as visual aids are concerned . . .' Lauren should listen especially carefully to this bit. But instead her eyes are sneaking over to the window where Jason is dancing.

He's waving his hand in the air and jiving about, as if he's auditioning for *Grease*. He used to do this at school too, and have the class in fits. And right then, Lauren lets out a squeal of laughter which she hastily turns into a rather high-pitched cough.

Her tutor looks at her, then asks, 'So how does that sound?'

'Oh, very good.' Her voice has risen about two octaves.

'Now, a few pointers for your presentation,' says her tutor. Go on, listen to this, Lauren tells herself. But her eyes seem to have a will of their own. And now . . . oh, look at him! He's only pulling at his shirt as if he's about to throw it off. It's then Lauren feels the great wave of laughter fighting to break free. And then, suddenly, it's out, erupting all over her tutor.

'I'm sorry,' she gasps.

Her tutor looks at Lauren, then spots Jason prancing in front of the window and says, 'I'm obviously wasting your time, and mine.'

'No, no,' begins Lauren.

But her tutor is already up and sweeping out of the staffroom. Immediately he's gone, Jason bounds in. 'You're evil,' cries Lauren, wiping the tears of laughter from her face. 'What must he think?'

Jason waves a dismissive hand. 'He looks like someone's just sat on his face.'

'But Jason, he was helping me. I've got to do this talk tomorrow which I'm being assessed on and I haven't a clue what to do. And it's not funny.'

'You'll be all right,' says Jason. 'You always have lots to say.'

Lauren gazes at him with both exasperation and affection. And as they walk out of the staffroom, she asks, 'And what do you want, anyway?'

'Nothing much, just to make mad, passionate love to you all night.'

'Jason!'

'Are you shocked by my depravity? Let me deprave you.'

'What are you on, today?'

He laughs. 'Today, I'm on such a charisma overload, that one look from me will set your hair on fire and I've been given free tickets for this new club tonight.'

'Oh, not tonight, Jason. I just told you, I've got to work.

He nods at a couple of guys in the entrance – Jason seems to know everyone in Cartford – then says, 'We needn't go until about eight o'clock,' then adds, 'I'll go on my own and get off with that girl who keeps wanting to put her tongue down my throat, Angelina, she's going to be a model for . . .'

'Hamster food,' interrupts Lauren. 'You dare go near her!'

He laughs. 'I'll pop round then, usual time.'

'No, Jason, not tonight, please.'

He looks offended. 'Not even for coffee?'

She hesitates. 'No, not tonight, if you don't mind. I think we're . . .'

'What?' He's not smiling now.

'We don't have to see each other every single night, do we?'

'Fine.' Then he says, 'I'd better get back to the shop,' and stalks off, without another word. Lauren stares after him. Should she go after him? But she does want an evening to herself. Is that so bad? And she has got so much work to do. In fact, she really is starting to fall behind.

As she walks past, a horn goes off. She immediately rushes over. 'Cathy, your halo shines so brightly these days. But I said not to wait, I'd get the bus.'

'I'm in no hurry to get home,' says Cathy grimly.

'Things bad?'

The car glides off. 'Not exactly bad, more like tiring. We're all trying so hard to be such a happy little family. Still, at least it's the wedding next week and then I'll have a few days to myself. Was old Barry any help then?'

'No, not really. In fact, it was a disaster.'

Cathy turns round sharply. 'Why?'

'Jason turned up, and started making faces in the window. Then he did his *Grease* dancing – you know.'

'I know. What a crack,' cries Cathy.

'No. It wasn't. I only ended up laughing in Barry's face, didn't I?'

Cathy gasps and smiles.

'Yes, and he was not happy and I still haven't

60

decided what I'm doing for my talk. So I'm really going to have to work tonight. Of course, when I asked Jason not to come round tonight, he wasn't best pleased. But he's got to understand that some nights I must work. I don't want to throw all my A levels away, do I?'

'No,' says Cathy, mildly.

'Anyway, at the moment I feel Jason and I are living in each other's pockets. No wonder my parents go on about him. And I do need some space.'

Cathy doesn't say anything for a moment, then she asks, 'Lauren, would you say you're in love with Jason?'

'I hate questions like that.'

'I know.' Cathy smiles, then says, 'Come on, tell me.'

Lauren breathes out slowly. 'In this time-frame, I love him.'

'What does that mean?'

'It means, that right now, I do. But move me on to another time-frame, like university, well, who knows . . . I'm too young to say I'm going to love someone, even Jason, forever, aren't I?'

'Yes, I suppose so,' says Cathy, faintly.

'Oh, Cathy, you're such a romantic.'

'No, I'm not.'

'Yes you are – a real little romantic. Anyway, one day you might marry Jez.'

61

Cathy shakes her head. 'To be honest, I doubt if I'll ever see Jez again. He hasn't written for ages. I don't think he'll ever come home.'

'Yes, he will and one day you might . . . just like Jason and I might! She leans forward. 'In fact, Jason and I probably will get married but not for a long time yet.'

Jason paces furiously around his bedroom. Years ago he painted all the walls in his bedroom black. But tonight, they are not black enough. From downstairs, he can hear scraps of conversation. His Aunt Lucifer, or someone, has come round. He's supposed to honour her with a guest appearance. But tonight, he can't talk to anyone. At any second, his head will explode. If only he knew why she did it. Why did Lauren turn him down tonight?

She says she's got to work. But no one works all night, do they? There's something else here. And the reason isn't difficult to see; she's getting bored with him. These last few evenings it has gone a bit flat, actually. Last night, especially, the conversation kept going dry. That's why Jason bought these tickets.

She's slipping away, isn't she? He clenches his fists. He's so frustrated, he could punch the walls. Once, years ago, he'd head-butted the wall. He had told Lauren about it but she just laughed and said, 'That explains a lot.'

62

'Lauren.' He yells the word aloud. What does he care if she stays in tonight? He'll go out tonight on his own and he'll pull . . . That Angelina came into the sports shop today. She's got amazing blonde hair, a bit like Becky's style only longer, and she's dead tall. She towered over everyone in the shop except Jason, of course. And she did give him the eye. He could be in there.

Instead, he's trapped in his room, willing the phone to ring and for Lauren to say, 'I'm missing you, please come round after all.' But now, it's twenty-five past ten. She's not going to ring, because she's not missing him, not at all.

He clenches his fists tighter and tighter. He's losing her, isn't he? And he hasn't a clue what to do. What can he do? Nothing, except hang on tighter.

4
Stolen From the Post

My dear Jez,

At last, a letter from you, or a postcard with a few squiggles on it, anyway. No, really it was lovely to hear from you. I was getting very impatient for news.

So you're back in Berlin again. Thanks for the address. But what's all this 'in case you remember me?' You might not think so but we all still miss you madly and we are looking forward to seeing you – when we see you. You say you should be home 'quite soon'. Can you be more definite?

You ask me about my mum's wedding. Well, it happened last week in Cartford Registry Office. Then there was a buffet lunch at which Giles asked everyone to be sure to leave the receipt slips with the presents, so he could take them all back if they weren't suitable. Some people even laughed. Mum looked so beautiful though, far, far, too good for him.

When she left for her honeymoon, both me and my sister cried and cried. (I thought it was mothers who were supposed to cry at weddings – not daughters. Never mind!!) Lauren and Jason (who came to the wedding) took us both out for a meal and I think my little sister's madly in love with Jason now.

Talking of Jason, he went into court today for my crime (though you are the only person who knows that last fact). Lauren, Mark and myself went along for moral support. It was all so solemn and seeing Jason gazing around with those quick, dark eyes, it really tugged at my heart but made me want to smile too. Anyway, he was fined two hundred and fifty pounds, slightly more than expected, (he can pay it off, twenty pounds a week) and I, of course, am insisting on paying every penny of it. In fact, this week I've increased my hours at the *Pizza Paradiso*. But I tell you, Jez, I hate that job so much. If there was anything better, I'd be in there right away but there's just nothing around.

I'm working really long shifts now and it's such a relief if someone even smiles at you. Most of the time people act as if you're invisible. So often I go up to a table and ask, 'Are you ready to order?' and everyone just carries on talking as if you're not there. The only time they notice you is when they

65

want to moan about something like, why haven't they got their free badges. The other day this guy looked up from the menu to say, 'I don't like pizzas'. I thought, so why come into a pizza place then?

Poor Becky's dead worried about her job. For today, this guy came in and just stood there in Becky's section like he was waiting for a bus. Becky was so busy she never saw him. Anyway, this guy only went and complained to the deputy manager. You see, you're supposed to greet a customer within thirty seconds of them entering the door and take their order within three minutes. So the manager's back tomorrow and Becky's got to go and see him and he's a real slimy toad. He's always putting his arm around the girls and massaging their necks and saying, 'We care about our staff.' Yet, he'll fire you for anything. He fired this girl last week for not being enthusiastic enough and someone else for complaining about the rota. Of course, Becky really needs the money.

In fact, she and Adam are working so hard now. This is when I wish I had lots of money. I'd love to give them some. So what else is new? Not much really. Mark's rushing about, in fact, he's the busiest of all of us now. He's organising a college trip to a club next week, which we're all going on. Oh yes, Lauren's asked me to go to Portugal with her and her parents. I said, 'What about Jason?' and she said that her parents weren't keen on Jason going with them and also, how she wants to have some fun!! (What can she mean!)

I must stop now. I hope you notice how, once again, I replied sooner than soonest. So write SOON, or even better, COME HOME.

Until then, may your shadow never grow shorter.
Much love,
Cathy xxx

September 17th

My dear Jez,

We're in uproar here. I've just shown everyone your postcard. You've written 'See you very soon' but how soon is 'very soon'? Why can't you be more specific? Would it kill you to give us a date?

Maybe you'll have left before this letter reaches you, but I feel like writing to someone and you're the lucky one. Anyway, you will have noticed that I'm back from Portugal (hope you got our post-cards). It was brilliant, except for the dead rat in the swimming pool. Lauren's dad found it there. I couldn't swim in the pool for a week after that. And no one knew what vegetarian means. But the people were friendly and everything was so relaxed and slow – if you go out for a meal, it takes at least four hours. You'd love it there. And you'd certainly appreciate the way everything closes at midday for a siesta.

In Portugal, Lauren met this guy called Doug.

He's twenty-four, quite intellectual, also a pretty good dancer. By the third week he always seemed to be around. I didn't mind him (he was always quite polite to me) and Lauren said, 'It's just fun'. But something in my bones told me this was not right – or am I just old-fashioned?

When we got home there was a message from Jason. It was quite funny, actually. First there was this heavy breathing, then Jason in this terrible French accent says, 'Lauren' then there's more deep breathing, following by 'Je t'aime baby'. Lauren smiled then said, 'End of freedom'. But when Jason turned up a couple of hours later, she was all over him and started telling me how much she'd missed him, so I don't know.

We went back to college on Monday and all our lecturers have been telling us how hard this year is going to be. Lauren is now going through these university prospectuses. I envy Lauren being so certain of what she wants. I'm not so sure if I want to go on to university. I've got this strange feeling of not knowing what I want. In fact, I'm going through this very unconfident phase, which is so annoying. I get nervous when I meet people and I talk too much, saying rather silly things. But I'm determined to get out of this phase and I keep pushing myself along. Like last Saturday, I went to this house-party with a girl from my English class, Adele. And the house was full of sexist, ignorant, narrow-minded males, so yes, it was quite a fun party. For about an hour anyway. After that I got so bored I left, just as a major row was breaking out as to who was going to sleep on which sofa.

Oh yes, bit of gossip about that party. Our least favourite English teacher, Grant, was there with Tricia Williams. They were kissing and everything. I couldn't believe they were so public. The real laugh was that they must have had an argument or something, because in the middle of the party, Tricia flounced off. She came back later though and they made up. I reckon Lauren is well out of all that, I really do.

As for everyone else, Adam's still working at the video shop. In fact, he seems virtually to live in there. He said he'll be taking his sleeping bag along soon! Becky's hoping to keep working at the *Pizza Paradiso* until the end of the month, or a bit longer if she can. She's still not showing very much (baby is due at the end of November) but she is looking very tired.

And finally, the hot news, Mark is standing for President of the Students' Union. As you know (I think) Mark was nominated for Vice-President but then the guy who was standing for President has been accused of fiddling the books, so he's out and because Mark's such a hard-working and skilful exec. member he's one of the two candidates for President. The election takes place on September

28th. Will you be home by then? *I do hope so*. Then we can all go out together and as Jason would say, 'have a riot'.

So hurry home. We're all missing you. Can't think why!

Much love,
Cathy xxx

5 An Election and an Emergency

There's just ten minutes left before voting for the post of student President ends. The result looks like being a very close one and both the candidates are still much in evidence. Paul Christie, a large, some might say 'porky-looking' guy in a tracksuit, has planted himself in front of the *Vote here* notice outside the hall. Some of his mates, also in tracksuits, hang noisily beside him.

Cathy and Lauren are standing just inside reception, handing out leaflets headed, MARK APPLETON.; HEADLINE POLICIES, while Mark paces around. Cathy's always liked Mark's jaunty, busy walk, with his head thrust forward as if he's waiting to run a race.

Mark spends an hour a day waxing down his curly hair, in an effort to give him a more mature look, yet his skin is still baby-soft and when he smiles, his teeth still take over his face. He looks fresh, sincere and very eager; you can almost see his tail wagging as he approaches you. Cathy's sure she would vote for him even if she didn't know him, and just about everyone in Mark's class said they'll definitely put a cross by his name. But it's all these floating voters Mark really needs to catch. Like the two girls he's just gone up to. She hears him say, 'Hi, I'm Mark Appleton and I'm standing for President of the Students' Union' – quick flash of teeth – 'can I just ask what you want out of the students' union?'

Meanwhile, beside her, Lauren is slipping her hand on to this guy's arm. 'So if you could just put your little cross by Mark's name.'

'Sure, okay,' he says, huskily.

'Thanks ever so much.' Her voice is now a sultry whisper. 'I'm so grateful.'

'That's all right, see you around then,' says the guy, smiling hopefully at Lauren. She tosses him a little smile in return, then murmurs, 'Not if I see you first.'

Cathy turns back to Mark, who is saying to the two girls, 'Yes, if you'd like a trip to Alton Towers, I think I could organise that. Thanks a lot, bye.' Then he bounces over to Cathy and Lauren. 'I'm agreeing to anything now. I'll be your friend, if you vote for me. It's terrible, really.'

'Everybody does it,' says Lauren, nodding over

at Mark's competitor. 'He's been promising parties every night.'

'And at least you stand for something,' says Cathy. 'He's got no ideas at all.'

'Trouble is,' says Mark, 'no one seems to read the leaflets. Maybe I should have made a video, then . . .' He's interrupted by Cathy calling out, 'Becky!' as Becky rushes into reception. 'Just made it,' she gasps.

Straight away, Mark notices she's put something on her face to make it glow. But it's made her skin turn an over-bright orange and only reminds Mark of the paleness she's trying to cover up.

'You shouldn't have bothered,' he says. That sounds ungrateful. 'I mean, it's out of your way.'

'I just thought, as I'm still a paid-up member of the student union, I'd do my duty.' She gives a breathless laugh. 'Only I couldn't get away from work. See you in a minute, then.' She speeds into the hall. Mark guesses coming back to college can't be a great experience for her.

'She's working too hard,' says Cathy. 'Because she's not getting any maternity benefit, she's still working full time at the *Pizza Paradiso*. Her mum's had a real go at her – and Adam – and so have I, but she's determined.'

'She's hiding it well, isn't she?' says Lauren. 'I mean, you'd never guess it's due in, what, six weeks?'

'She doesn't look well though,' declares Mark. 'She should be at home.' And when Becky re-appears from doing her duty, he tells her, 'You don't look at all well.'

'Thanks, Mark,' says Becky.

'But you don't,' he says. 'And everyone thinks you're doing too much.'

'Don't you start,' says Becky. 'It's bad enough my mum flapping about. I'd be okay if it weren't for this awful indigestion. I blame my mum for that. Last night, she cooked this roast dinner and sat there watching me eat it. Then, at seven o'clock this morning she brings in this huge breakfast, which I really couldn't face, but she kept popping back, going, "Have you eaten it yet?" And she gives me a lunch box every day now . . . Do I look really awful?'

'No, not at all,' chorus Lauren and Cathy.

'Mark, babe, good luck,' cries a voice. It's Vicki, a girl from his English group.

'Thanks, I'll need it,' he says.

She gives an exclamation of amazement: 'Oh Becky, I haven't seen you for ages. And how long before . . . you know?'

'Not long,' says Becky, her voice tightening rapidly.

'Oooh,' Vicki coos, 'that's really exciting.' She looks as if she'd like to ask more but Becky's whole body-language says, 'Don't speak to me.'

74

'Goodbye for now, then, Becky,' she says.

'She talks like a hairdresser,' says Lauren. 'Everything's really exciting or really sweet. She thinks she's so lovely, too. But she's got that horrible, pinched doll's mouth . . . don't let her get to you, Becky.'

'Oh, I won't. It's just I don't really want to talk to anyone. Afterwards, I won't care. But I hate the way they just stare at me, as if I've turned into some kind of freak. Still, I'd better go, I told them I'd only be ten minutes, so they'll probably be screaming for me.'

'Are you still on for the fair tonight?' asks Mark.

'Yes, I'm looking forward to it.' She turns to Mark, 'When will you know, then?'

'Soon. Voting should close about now. Then I've got half-an-hour to wait.'

Becky smiles sympathetically. 'Nervous?'

'More than a bit. Wish me luck, then.'

'Oh, I do. Buckets of it.'

'If I win, I'll drop in and tell you. If I don't, you'll see me hanging from the ceiling.'

'You're going to win. I know it. Adam voted, didn't he?'

'Yes,' says Mark. 'Came in about an hour ago.'

'He said he would. Right, see you all tonight, then,' she smiles. 'And I'll see you soon, Mark.'

'Don't rush,' Mark calls after her. Then he says, 'She looks terrible.'

'And I'm sure you really cheered her up by telling her,' says Lauren.

'I wanted to shock her into looking after herself,' replies Mark.

'She won't give up her job,' says Cathy. 'She says she wants her baby to have the best chance and that means earning as much money as she can. Even Adam can't talk her out of it.'

The hall door opens and Royston, the current President, says something to Paul Christie and his supporters, then comes over to Mark. 'Voting is now closed, Mark. We've had quite a lot of interest. We hope to have the result before afternoon lessons start.' Clearly enjoying the suspense of it all, he adds, 'I know exactly what you're going through. Last year, at this time when I was waiting . . .'

'Tell us your life-story, why don't you,' mutters Lauren. Royston had been a hard-working president but one who enjoyed the sound of his own endless ramblings and whose manner was that of a well-meaning vicar.

After he's gone, Lauren says, 'Every time he speaks I keep getting distracted by his zits. That guy has got acne in a major way.'

'He can't help that,' says Cathy. 'Just don't ever let your speeches be as boring . . .'

'You needn't worry about that,' says Mark, 'because it's a fact that people always vote for the taller person in elections.'

76

'Come on, you're getting all droopy,' says Lauren. 'Time we went for a walk.'

So she and Cathy go into town with Mark, while he babbles on about how being President would be very time-consuming and really, he'd be better off if he loses. But when they return to reception, Mark says softly, 'I want it so badly, you know, and it's not just having the title, though I'd like it. I know you've got to be committed, really put yourself about and I'd enjoy doing that. Do you think I've got a chance?'

Cathy squeezes his hand. 'If there's any justice, you'll get in with a landslide.'

The hall door is now open and chairs have been laid out. Students are trickling in and Royston is buzzing about. He tells Mark, 'I've sent someone into the refectory to say we're going to announce the new President. It was very close,' he adds. Is this his way of preparing Mark for defeat? 'You're on the stage,' adds Royston, before rushing off. So Mark's humiliation is to be in full view.

'Remember, you're going to win,' whispers Lauren, as she and Cathy take their places in the second row. Mark edges on to the stage, where his rival, Paul, is already seated. Mark immediately extends his hand. 'Good luck, mate,' he says.

'And to you,' replies Paul, dutifully.

'Nothing more we can do now, is there?' says Mark.

'Not a thing,' agrees Paul. They exchange 'we're such good sports' smiles, while Mark thinks, you've been to one committee meeting this year and if you get elected, just because you're hunky and started a basketball team that wins every match and you're a foot taller than me . . . Still, what can Mark do? Nothing, except practise his plucky loser smile. At least Mark's got this far. At school he was just a bit of a joke. He seemed to spend most of his time gazing into other people's eyes for a glimpse of himself. He was just like a hologram person. You could walk right through him. There was nothing to him. Or so he thought.

But all the time, tucked deep inside him . . . it's as if Mark's found this treasure chest. And every time he digs down he discovers something else about himself. There's much more to him than he ever suspected. He's quite a deep person, really.

Royston clears his throat, twice, and tells the packed hall, 'This is my last day as President.'

'Good,' calls a voice.

'And my final talk is to announce my successor,' he pauses, then continues, 'I remember . . .'

'When I was born,' someone hisses; Royston's long, rambling speeches almost demand heckles. This time, even Royston takes the hint.

'The votes were as follows . . . '

Mark, sitting with his arms and legs tightly crossed, hardly dares to listen.

'Mark Appleton, 841 votes.'

There's clapping and Mark's heart seems to thump out its own applause. That's a good vote but is it good enough?

'Paul Christie,' Royston pauses dramatically, '821 votes. So you can see, it was very close, but I declare Mark Appleton is our new President.' All at once, Royston is extending his hand to Mark, inviting him to speak. Mark doesn't remember getting to his feet and he seems just to float over to the podium. Then he looks over to the audience. At that moment, the hall door creaks open and Jason spins into view. There are a couple of spare seats but Jason doesn't attempt to move towards any of them. Instead, he just stands at the back, with his arms folded, looking like a bodyguard. But Mark catches his eye and Jason gives him one of his rare, beaming smiles. And right then, Mark's flying into orbit. For he's done it, hasn't he? He's the President. He can make things happen. Now he's got to deliver.

'First of all,' he says, 'I want to thank my brilliant rival, Paul, who I look forward to working with on the committee.' There's a loud applause for the loser. Then Mark says, 'And, thanks for voting for me. If you read my sheet, you'll know I've got a few, what I call, headline policies. Firstly, all the loos stink, well the men's do, anyway. They've got to be cleaned.' Applause starts up. Mark raises his hand, 'There's more. The refectory is open for all of two seconds. It should be open all day.' More applause. 'We're going to have another pool table and this time, one that doesn't get smashed up.' There's a loud cheer from the back of the hall. 'And I'm going to keep organising events. I want this college to be the centre for parties,' loud applause now, 'and for talks,' rather quieter applause, 'and for charity events and we're going to have a newsletter.' Mark's light, rapid voice whirls on. 'Also, I want surgeries, where you can put questions to the principal. I tell you, Cartford College is going to be the college where things happen.'

There's wild applause now, some people are even standing up. Mark stares at them in wonderment. He's really got them going, hasn't he? But can he do all that? No time to worry now, for they're lapping around him, shaking his hand, patting him on the back, calling out, 'Congratulations'.

'You were brilliant,' cries Cathy, flinging her arms around him.

'Almost made me wish I'd voted for you,' quips Lauren.

'Where's Jason?' asks Mark.

'Jason?' asks Lauren.

'Yeah, he was here, standing at the back.'

'Oh,' Lauren's immediately looking round. Sometimes Lauren seems really casual about Jason, almost as if he's a bit of a nuisance, or so it appears to Cathy. Yet, other times, like now, Lauren becomes flushed and excited, just by hearing his name.

But Jason is nowhere to be seen. 'I guess he saw what he wanted to see – which is you being President – then shot off again,' says Cathy.

'He might have stayed to say hello to us,' says Lauren. Cathy looks at her curiously. Yesterday, Lauren had been moaning on about how Jason never left her home before midnight.

As they walk down the steps into reception, the whole place seems to echo with 'Congratulations, Mark,' and 'I voted for you, Mark.'

'It's amazing really, isn't it,' says Mark. 'I was just going to stand as one of the committee and then when the chance to be President turned up, I thought, if you're going to be a bear, be a grizzly . . . We must go and tell Becky in a minute.'

Royston is panting behind them. 'The Principal has asked if you could meet him for coffee tomorrow, around half past ten.'

Mark rolls his shoulders a bit. 'I think I could manage that. Yes, tell him I'll he along. Hear that, Lauren, Cathy.'

'We heard,' says Lauren. She turns to Cathy. 'Do you think that smile's ever going to leave his face?'

*

'Scream if you want to go faster,' his red face lurches over Cathy. But Cathy, who is sitting right back in the waltzer, can only manage a thin scream. Lauren, however, leans forward and gives a far more ear-shattering performance, which is applauded by Adam, who is squashed between them.

'Hold tight then,' cries the scarecrow man, puffing excitedly. 'The scarecrow man' is what Lauren and Cathy christened him, years ago now. For as long as they've come to the fair, he's been here in his trilby hat, woollen waistcoat, green trousers and surprisingly trendy ankle wellies, with the socks peering over the top. And he always pushed the girls extra hard if they screamed – like now.

Cathy closes her eyes. She loves the waltzer and she hates it. Suddenly, Lauren falls forward, screaming and laughing. Cathy can feel herself being pulled forward too. She closes her eyes again, while her head rolls around furiously. Any second now it'll take off and she'll just spin into infinity. But then, Lauren's nudging Cathy and saying, 'You can open your eyes now,' and the three of them are stumbling over to Becky, who smiles enviously at them. In her old town, they had this brilliant waltzer which had all these flashing laser beams, she was always going on it. But tonight, she can only stand and watch and smile, like some elderly relative, because – well – it's really annoying, actually.

For, earlier this evening, Becky had been okay-ish. And she'd gone round to Cathy's and they'd got ready together, had a nice gossip and Becky had felt relaxed and happy. But then, just as they were leaving for the fair, Becky got this terrible ache in her stomach again. She didn't tell anyone, as being ill all the time – which she seems to be now – is so boring and she hoped the pain would go away. And it does, for a few minutes, but then it comes back worse than ever.

She's also got this horrible sicky feeling. She keeps wanting to go to the loo and generally, she feels so cross with herself. Other women carry on working until just before their baby is born. And Becky's got weeks, five or six, anyway, before the baby is due. Yet most of the time now she feels so tired and ill and pathetic, while everyone around her, of course, is blazingly healthy. Now Adam is asking, 'Not feeling so good?'

'No, I'm okay. I'm fine.' If she talks about it, she only feels worse. Think positive. She's leaning against the waltzer because she feels dizzy if she stands up for too long. What is happening to her? And why is everyone staring at her so anxiously? They're not helping. It's quite a relief when Lauren declares, 'Here come the riflemen.'

Jason and Mark are steaming towards them,

grinning triumphantly, their arms full of bright green teddy bears.

'What did you get all these for?' asks Lauren.

'Jason just kept on shooting bullseyes and winning them at the shooting gallery,' says Mark. 'It was brilliant. Finally, they sent for this fat old bloke, in a peaked cap, with tattoos all up his arm.'

'Reckoned he was Mr Hard Man,' says Jason. 'I could have seen him off, but I thought . . .'

'I'm glad you didn't,' interrupts Lauren. 'Imagine getting into a fight over something so truly disgusting as this.' Jason hands her a teddy bear. 'No, take it away. What do I want one of those for? Honestly, how old are you two? Were you really made President of the Student Union today, Mark?' Jason and Mark's faces fell.

'I think they're rather cute, in a tacky sort of way,' says Becky, taking one.

Cathy takes one too. 'And it's all part of the fun of the fair, isn't it?' She sniffs hard. 'Will you smell those fried onions. Normally, I hate that smell but here, mixed up with candy floss and diesel and all the other fair smells, mmm, beautiful.' She sniffs again, then says, 'I smoked my first – and last – cigarette at the fair, remember, Lauren?'

Lauren smiles, 'I remember, you couldn't inhale it. I kept saying, take it through the nose.'

'Coming here used to be the highlight of the

entire year, didn't it?' says Adam. 'It was like the first time you were allowed out on your own.'

'And there was always a fight by the slot-machines. Every year,' says Mark.

'This old fair's shrunk a bit, though,' says Jason. 'Remember the ghost train? I loved that.'

'Oh, that was crap,' says Lauren, 'especially that stupid skeleton that used to jump out at people.'

'No, I liked that,' says Jason.

'So did I,' agrees Cathy. 'And I used to like going through all those little flaps.'

'Enough reminiscing,' cries Lauren. 'Let's get down and do it . . . the big wheel next, I think, Cathy?'

'Okay,' says Cathy, slowly. 'I do like it, except when you get to the top and you can see over to the river. I hate that bit . . .'

But Lauren's already sprinting away.

'Wait for us,' calls Jason, taking Cathy's hand. She looks at him in pleased surprise.

Then Cathy turns back, 'Come on Mark, Adam, you're not getting out of this and Becky, I don't suppose?'

Becky shakes her head sadly. 'But you go, Adam.'

'No, I'll stay with you,' says Adam.

'And so will I,' says Mark, unexpectedly.

'You don't have to stay with me,' says Becky, feeling distinctly tetchy. She's ruining the fair for everyone else. It would have been better if she'd stayed at home. Her mum said she shouldn't go. But that only made Becky all the more keen. She breathes hard. She's got this awful backache now. How many more weeks of this misery has she got left? If she'd known before – but now she's just being cowardly.

'Look at Cathy's face,' cries Mark, pointing. 'She's really wetting herself.' Mark and Adam wave and laugh and Becky smiles dutifully. Then, all at once, the backache is shooting all over her body. She's exploding with pain. She creases over, lets out a sharp scream of pain, then another. Adam's beside her and he's asking her something but she can't reply because she's breathing too hard. All she can do is scream again.

But she hears Mark say, 'We must get an ambulance. I'll ring for one.' Then Mark's jumping about, yelling, 'Adam, where's the nearest phone?' They gape at each other. Both their brains seem to have seized up, until Mark cries, 'About half a mile away we passed one, didn't we?' At once, he's racing furiously down the road. Just seeing Becky collapse like that; even now he's got his teeth tightly clenched to stop them from chattering.

Looming ahead is the phone, only there's someone using it. A guy about his own age, only bigger, of course. Mark senses he's talking to a girl. But Mark can't wait, can't hesitate. He pulls the glass door open, taps the guy on the shoulder and mumbles apologetically, 'Need the phone now. It's an emergency.' The guy turns round and gives Mark a sharp, dismissive glance. Come on, be authoritative, Mark tells himself. 'I'm sorry mate, this is an emergency. I've got to ring for an ambulance.' Then Mark raises his hand as if he's about to grab the phone. The guy mumbles something, slams the receiver down, then takes a couple of steps back. 'Thanks, I won't be long,' says Mark. 'You don't know the number of the hospital? No, okay.'

Mark scrambles through the telephone book and is already dialling when he hears his name being called. Cathy bursts into the now crowded phone box. 'Change of plan. Jason's driving Becky to the hospital. Will you just tell the hospital we're on our way.' Before Mark can reply, a voice on the line is crackling, 'Cartford General Hospital'.

'This is an emergency, Becky – his mind goes blank. 'Edwards,' prompts Cathy, and Mark continues, 'Becky Edwards is being driven to your hospital. She's expecting a baby in a few weeks and she's just collapsed at the fair.'

'Is she booked to have the baby here?'

'Yes,' says Mark.

'And her name is Becky Edwards.'

'Yes.'

'And how is she coming?'

'By car. Some friends are bringing her.'

'Right, we'll have a team waiting for her, Mr . . .'

'Mark Appleton.' He puts the phone down, breathing hard. 'Thanks mate,' he says to the guy. Then he and Cathy sprint back to the fair, just as Adam and Jason are helping Becky into Jason's car.

Mark rushes over. 'Becky.' He doesn't know why he calls her name out. Her face is ghostly white but she gives a tiny smile, then in a wisp of a voice asks, 'My mum, can you ring my mum?'

'Yeah, sure I will, as soon as we get to the hospital. Anything else you want?'

But Becky has already sprawled back in her seat, her face twisted with pain. Lauren gets in beside Becky, while Jason and Adam sit in the front. Lauren gently puts her coat over Becky. Adam flings his jacket off and hands it to Becky. 'Have this too,' he says.

'She can have my jacket if she likes,' says Jason, though not particularly enthusiastically.

'No, just got to keep her warm,' says Lauren. 'Can you try and take some deep breaths, Becky?'

Becky gives a groan in reply.

'She's got to keep the oxygen going round her body,' explains Lauren. 'That's what they told us in Biology, anyway.'

'I think she's all right,' murmurs Cathy. 'Just get to the hospital as soon as you can, Jason. We'll follow behind.'

Jason starts the car up, while Adam turns round

and holds Becky's hand. 'It won't be long now, my darling. It won't be long.'

When Jason pulls into the hospital he sees a nurse and an ambulanceman waiting outside with a wheelchair. He signals to the nurse, a comfortable-looking, grey-haired woman, who rushes forward.

Jason gets out and opens the back door. Becky is hunched in the corner, holding on to Adam's hand. The nurse bears down and says, 'It's all right Becky, your friends have got you to the hospital, so now just leave it to us.' Then the nurse helps the ambulanceman get Becky into the wheelchair. Adam kneels down and kisses Becky on the forehead.

'Are you dad?' asks the nurse. Her tone is friendly.

'Yes, I'm dad,' says Adam.

'Well, I'm Nurse Stevenson. Would you like to come with me.' Then the nurse turns to Lauren and Jason. 'And could you two go to the waiting room.' She doesn't wait for an answer and Becky is whisked away.

Cathy drives into view. She parks her car behind Jason's. She and Mark get out.

'We've got to go to the waiting room,' exclaims Lauren. 'I'm sure Becky would want us to be with her.'

'I expect there's too many of us,' says Cathy.

Jason lets the girls lead the way into the hospital. He hangs back and mutters to Mark, 'I really hate hospitals.'

'I'm not too keen on them either,' says Mark. 'When I was ten I had my tonsils out and I remember the baths were made of steel and always really cold and the food trolley smelt of cabbage.'

'I've never had to stay in hospital,' says Jason. 'I've never been ill, really. But hospitals give me this really bad feeling.' He shudders. 'Hate them.' Then he adds, 'Did you see that nurse's teeth? They're rank, all brown.'

Inside the hospital, the four of them are guided to their waiting room. Just up the corridor they spot Adam, standing outside one of the rooms. 'Any news?' calls Lauren.

'No, they just took Becky in there and asked me to wait,' he calls back.

A nurse swishes past. 'Would you mind waiting inside, please. We will keep you informed.'

'You'd better,' murmurs Lauren.

Once inside, Mark makes for the pay phone. 'I'll ring Becky's mum.' Everyone else hovers uncertainly.

'Anyone want a coffee?' asks Jason.

Cathy and Lauren shake their heads.

'I don't either,' says Jason.

'This is so awful, being stuck in here like this,' declares Lauren.

'We may as well sit down,' says Cathy.

But both Lauren and Jason continue pacing around the room. Mark turns round from the phone. 'There's no answer. I bet she's in her hut, writing. She says she can't hear the phone from there.'

'We'd better drive round,' says Jason and he's already at the door of the waiting room.

'Yeah, okay,' says Mark.

'We won't be long,' says Jason.

'Do you think you should see Adam's parents too?' Cathy calls after them.

Mark considers this. 'No, not yet.'

Adam is still waiting outside. They walk up to him. Jason asks, 'How long are they going to keep you out here, then?'

Adam shrugs his shoulders.

'We're just going to get Becky's mum,' says Jason.

'There was no answer from her phone,' says Mark. 'So we reckon she's probably in her writing hut.'

'Yeah, right, thanks,' says Adam. 'And thanks, for driving us here and . . .'

'All part of the service,' says Jason.

The door opens and Nurse Stevenson appears. 'Well, Adam, the baby is on its way.' All three of them stare incredulously at her.

'But it's not due for five weeks yet,' whispers Adam.

The nurse smiles faintly. 'Babies decide to come when they want to come.'

'Is Becky all right?' asks Mark.

'Yes. And we will do our best for her.' Her tone becomes formal. 'Adam, do you wish to be with Becky now?'

'Yes,' says Adam firmly. Jason shudders inwardly. He remembers that film about childbirth they had to watch at school. It looked pretty messy to him.

'Right, if you'd like to come with me, please.'

Jason and Mark start to back away. 'We'll go and tell the girls, then we'll get Becky's mum. Good luck mate,' says Jason.

'Yeah, all the best,' calls Mark.

Adam is ushered into a small ante-room where the nurse hands him a green gown and a mask. His hands fumble as he tries to do the mask up. Suddenly, he hasn't got any strength in his fingers at all.

'They are a bit tricky,' says the nurse. 'Can I help?'

Then Adam follows her into a much larger room where Becky is lying, with her legs flexed, beneath a glaring white light, like a giant spotlight. Her face is drenched with sweat and her hair looks as if she's just been swimming. She is trembling and giving little whimpers of pain. Then she suddenly screams. The sound cuts right through him. He walks past the mysterious chrome machines and towards a doctor and two nurses, who are hovering around Becky.

In his haste to get to her, he knocks over the stool by her bed. Blushing slightly, he picks the stool up, then sits down beside her, immediately taking both her hands in his. They're soaking wet, but she squeezes his hand so tightly, it feels as if she's going to break his fingers. Her face seems smaller, flatter, but her eyes are wide and scared.

The nurse says, 'See, Becky, Adam is here now. It's all right Adam, the baby's head is showing, so it won't be long now.' Her voice is reassuring. 'Now Becky, I want you to listen to what I'm saying, as this is very important. When I say push, I want you to push as hard as you can. All right? But when I tell you not to push, you must stop immediately and pant, just like a dog would. Do you understand, Becky?'

Very slowly, Becky moves her head.

'And, Adam, do you understand these instructions?'

'Yes, I do.'

'Good. Now Becky, I want you to push as hard as you can . . . Yes, that's it, as hard as you can.'

'Listen Cathy, listen,' says Lauren excitedly. 'You

must hear it, too.' She and Cathy are waiting in the corridor outside the labour room. Cathy is really straining to hear now. 'No, I can't . . .' then a smile takes over her face. 'Yes, I do. I do.' They both hug each other.

'I told you,' says Lauren.

'But it was such a tiny little cry,' says Cathy.

'Well, what do you expect,' says Lauren. 'How would you feel at being suddenly pushed out into a strange, new world? I wonder if it's a boy or a girl. If only we could be in there. We should be in there.'

'It's a lovely little boy,' says the nurse.

Adam stares at the baby cradled in the nurse's arms; he's more than a bit disappointed, actually. For it looks so strange. Its face appears to be covered in white lard, for a start. And he looks so shrivelled, like a tiny old man. But this is his son. Adam's heart hammers excitedly, as he repeats the words over in his head; this is his son.

Becky raises her hands. 'Can I hold him,' she gasps.

'Not right now,' says the nurse. 'He is premature and must go straight into the incubator.'

'But he will be all right?' Adam's voice rises.

'We will do our very best for him, Adam,' she says.

6 *Thomas*

Adam wheels Becky through the doorway. Her mum and the nurse follow behind. 'Now, this is our Special Care Baby Unit,' says the nurse, in her bright, reassuring tone. 'And the first thing you'll probably notice is how hot it is. People often say it's like a greenhouse in here.'

They are fitted with masks, while all around them they can hear strange beeps and hums from the machines.

'Where's Thomas?' asks Becky, impatiently. It was about four o'clock this morning that she and Adam decided on a name. After they'd named him Becky thought, now he's got a name he'll pull through, he's got something to hang on to. Nothing can happen to him now.

The nurse pushes Becky down towards the end of the room. And there is Thomas, just inches

95

away from his parents, yet trapped inside his incubator, his cage.

'Thomas's changed colour,' cries Becky. 'He's pink now, that's a good sign, isn't it?' She and Adam look up at the nurse but she doesn't answer them.

They turn back to Thomas. The ventilator tube pulses up and down, lifting his tiny chest as it pumps oxygen into his lungs.

'Look at him,' cries Adam, for Thomas is moving his legs. Becky's eyes never leave Thomas now. But Adam has to keep turning away. 'Look at him,' says Becky suddenly as Thomas starts waving his fingers around, almost as if he were signalling to them from behind his glass wall.

'We'll soon have you out of there,' whispers Becky.

'Just keeping pushing,' says Adam. 'He's moving his legs again now, that's another good sign, isn't it?'

Later, Lauren and Cathy come in too. Lauren hangs back slightly, suddenly shy and a little scared, while Cathy gazes at Thomas in wonderment. 'Look at his tiny fingernails,' she cries. 'And oh, look at him trying to kick his legs.'

'He's kicking all the time. In fact, Becky and I think he's got the makings of a footballer,' says Adam, with a lightness he does not feel. 'Star player for Arsenal.'

'You mean Spurs, don't you?' replies Lauren.

'He'll play for them all,' says Becky.

Outside, Cathy says, 'He's a beautiful baby, isn't he?'

'Yes, he is,' says Lauren.

'What do you think?' Cathy can't bear even to ask it. 'Do you think . . . Thomas . . . has got a chance . . . ?'

'I don't know,' says Lauren flatly. Then she says, 'Can we get away for awhile, see how Mark got on with the Principal or something? I just need a bit of fresh air and yet, I feel awful, just walking away.'

Cathy links her arm. 'I could do with some fresh air too,' she says.

Then, as they start to walk away, Lauren says, 'What got me was the way he kept moving about all the time, didn't he. It was as if he didn't know how helpless he was.'

'He's a fighter all right,' murmurs Cathy, 'like his parents.'

Becky stirs. She must have dozed off for a while. She sits up, looking around her. It seems funny not to see Adam sitting by her bed. Or her mum, smiling anxiously down on her. Where have they gone? Now she remembers; Adam's mum and brother turned up at the hospital and Adam went to see them. Her mum must have gone too.

But that was two hours ago now. Or was it?

Maybe she's only been asleep for a few minutes. She sinks down again. Her back is whingeing away and she feels cold and shivery. She wishes someone would come and talk to her and take her to see Thomas. She doesn't like this silence. It's too loud.

She half closes her eyes again. Oh, hurry up, someone. Then she hears footsteps. She opens her eyes and there's Adam, her mum and the nurse. Before they say anything she knows and she doesn't want to hear them say it. So she cries, 'He's gone, hasn't he?'

Her mum says, 'His poor little lungs just weren't expanding properly . . . and he put up such a fight, didn't he?'

'We did everything we could, Becky,' says the nurse. Then she adds, 'Would you like to see him?'

Becky catches Adam's eye. He looks stunned and bewildered. Then he turns away as if to say, 'Don't ask me to make this decision.'

'Yes, I would,' says Becky. Becky's eyes turn again to Adam. But he can't seem to look at her. And in the end, it is Becky's mum who perches on the stool beside her. 'There are no words, are there?' says her mum. It's funny, for the last few hours, Becky's been clinging on to words and phrases which, even now, are running around in her head: where there's life there's hope. Never say die. No, there are no words. For all the words she chanted have let her down.

Now the nurse is walking slowly towards her, carrying Thomas wrapped in his white shawl, his skin a strange dark pink. More than anything else, Becky had longed to hold him. But only now, now when he's . . . Or at least, that's what they told her. That's what they think.

But look at him, lying in her arms, so beautiful, so perfect. Perhaps if she breathes on him, one of his fingers might start to move again. Or maybe if he feels how much she loves him one of his eyes will flutter open. Earlier, they'd lowered the side of the incubator and let her hold Thomas's hand. He'd gripped on to her with surprising tightness, as if he didn't want to let her go. But now, no one can waken him. Not even his mother. He's there in her arms and yet he's as far away from her as it's possible to be. Just where is he now? Growing up in some alternative universe?

One day, when she's an old, old lady and dying, will he be waiting there for her, all grown up? She kisses him on the forehead. Last time she'd touched him he felt soft and warm. Now, his skin's so cold. She lets out a gasp.

Her eyes search for Adam. He catches her gaze for a second, then turns away. Suddenly, he can't look her in the eye.

'Adam, you hold Thomas.'

'No, no, no,' he pushes his hand up. So Becky

continues to cradle her baby until the nurse says, 'Time to say goodbye now, Becky.'

Becky immediately tries to hold Thomas tighter. Only he's so light, it's as if she were trying to pull a piece of air towards her. Try as she might, she can't hold on to him.

'He's so beautiful,' murmurs her mum.

'Did you hear that, Thomas,' cries Becky. Your granny said you were beautiful and you are, the most beautiful baby in the world.'

The nurse is hovering over Becky now. Becky clasps Thomas to her one last time. 'I'm not saying goodbye,' she whispers, 'because I'll never forget you.'

'Adam, come on, open this door please,' cries his mother.

'But I'm all right.'

'Adam, open the door . . . please.'

Adam slowly gets to his feet. His head spins for a moment. It feels as if he's sprung up in the middle of the night, not ten o'clock in the morning.

He unlocks his bedroom door and his mum rushes in, hesitates for a moment, then plunges over to his curtains. With one tug she opens them as wide as they will go. Then she exclaims, 'Come on Adam, you've got to get dressed, you've not got much time.'

He falls back on top of the bed. 'I'm not going,' he says, shortly.

'But you can't not go to . . .' but his mum can't finish the sentence, can't add, to your son's funeral.

Adam closes his eyes. Inside himself there's now this giant knot, which every so often gets pulled so tightly it shakes all the life out of him. Sometimes he can hardly breathe, it squeezes him so tightly. He feels that now, just thinking about Thomas and Becky and . . . he should go. Of course he should. But he can't. No more. He just wants to be left alone now.

'Leave me alone, Mum. All of you. Is that too much to ask?'

'No, Adam,' says his mother. 'You must . . .'

'I don't know what you're so worried about,' he cries, his pain making him want to lash out. 'This proves you were right. God has punished Becky and me, hasn't he?' Adam can't help thinking this too. That's why he wants his mum to deny it. But she doesn't say anything, just stares at him in horror. 'Come on,' he cries, 'you never wanted this baby, did you?'

'No,' says his mum, backing away from him. 'But that doesn't mean we wanted this. A life is a life . . . and life is always sacred. Please believe me, Adam. I didn't want this.' She's pleading with him. And Adam doesn't think he can bear it. Especially, as deep down, he can feel sorry for his parents. In

101

their way, they've tried, haven't they? And yet, with
Adam, it's just one crisis after another. They must
be asking themselves what they've done to deserve
all this. Thank goodness they've got Reuben, the
good and faithful son who never fouls up and is,
even now, downstairs in his dark suit, rallying
around and generally being supportive.

'It's not your fault, Mum,' Adam says. 'It's me,
all me.' Then softly, tiredly, 'Please, just leave me
alone.'

Downstairs comes the sharp metallic ring of the
doorbell and Reuben calls, 'I'll go.' Normally, his
mum would be downstairs to see who it was. But
today, she just stands staring at him, frowning with
concentration.

'You must talk to Becky,' she says. 'Today of all
days. She's rung twice already.'

Adam sighs. 'Believe me, Mum, it's better this
way. It really is.'

His mum edges closer to him. Adam thinks she's
going to touch him but she doesn't, not quite. He
can see her struggling to find some way of reaching
him. But he's so far away from her. No words can
travel that distance. So in the end, the only sound is
the rain pattering on the window and then footsteps
coming up the stairs.

Reuben is standing in the doorway and saying,
rather uncertainly, 'And here's Becky.'

At once, Adam's mother goes over to her. With

one glance, she takes in the seventeen-year-old mother, all in black. Then her arms are around Becky and then they are clutching each other, not needing to say anything. Until, finally, his mum says, 'I'll leave you two, then,' closing the door behind her.

Becky hovers by the edge of his bed. 'Hello, Adam.' She says it quite shyly, as if they've just been introduced. By Adam's bed is a photograph of Becky. She's posing a bit, actually, doing her sultry smile, her hair arranged around her. She looks gorgeous and light years away from the deathly pale girl standing before him with eyes that look as if they're sinking into her head. She looks very ill and tired; she even looks smaller. Can sadness make you shrink? Whatever, he's done this to her. Now, that knot in his stomach is being pulled so tightly, he thinks he'll explode.

'I'm not going,' he cries. She doesn't answer. 'I'm not going to the funeral . . . I can't and do you know why?' The words are tearing out of him. 'Because if I do, something terrible will happen. Maybe, someone else will die. They say things go in threes, don't they. I don't know. But I'm bad luck, a jinx. Just look at my first girlfriend. A few months with me and she dies in a car crash on a Sunday afternoon. I only saw her the night before and she was just so happy. That's what I remember about her. She always made me laugh. And then

103

she goes and gets herself killed. But compared to you, she had a lucky escape.

'Just look at all the misery I've brought on you. Go on, look at it. One disaster after another. And it will go on like that.' He's shouting now. 'So go now, Becky, run away, while you can. Get out!' He flings open the door. 'Get out,' he repeats. And those sobs he's tried to bury down his throat start escaping, almost choking him with their force.

'Adam.'

'No, Becky. Just go, please.' He buries his head in his hands. 'Mark will be at the funeral. He'll look after you. He's the one for you, really. I snatched you away from him. Go to Mark.'

'Adam, please,' she puts her arm on to his. He tries to pull it away but he can't. 'Don't leave me now,' she whispers. 'I need you so much.'

He stumbles to his feet. His head feels as if it's about to split open. 'Can't you understand, there's nothing else inside me. I've got nothing left to give you. The night I saw our baby, well, that just finished me. That was my final screw-up.' He's standing by his door now. She walks over to him.

'Adam, it's not your fault.'

'But he's gone, Becky. Our baby's gone. All those months of struggle, all those hassles, all that planning, and for what? He's gone.'

'No, he's not,' says Becky, quickly. 'People never die when they live on in the hearts of those they've

104

left behind.' She's speaking so fast, she sounds as if she's reciting something she's learnt. 'Thomas is not gone, not while we remember him. That's why I've kept all his baby clothes, his little crib, everything we've bought. Mum wanted to get rid of them but I said, 'No, I want to keep it all because,' she stops and gazes into Adam's face as if searching for the reason, 'because he did live – he bloomed for a day, as my mum said – and I never want to forget that.'

There is silence again. Behind her words he can hear so much confusion and pain. And he knows their sounds, because they are in his head too.

He slumps down on to the side of his bed. 'I often think of him, you know,' he says softly. 'Sometimes I can see him so clearly. I still can't believe how tiny he was and yet he was perfect, wasn't he? I wish I'd held him that night. I wanted to, so much. I wanted to say goodbye to him, but I couldn't. Now I really wish I'd done that.'

Becky sits down on the edge of his bed beside him and from her suit pocket she takes out a gold locket. 'I've been keeping this for you. Here, take it, open it.'

In a kind of trance he opens it up and then lets out a cry. Inside the locket is a wisp of hair. She says, 'I asked the nurse. I thought you'd want it to . . .'

He gazes at the wisp of hair, as the tears rush

down his face. Finally he looks up. 'Becky, don't go,' he says.

Cathy gazes at the clouds racing across the sky. This morning, she'd woken to the sound of rain beating against her window and the day had looked grey and misty. Just the right weather for a funeral, Cathy had thought.

But they came out of the church to pale, white sunshine, and as the pitifully small coffin was lowered into the ground, sunlight glinted on it. And there are so many wreaths: in the centre is the one she, Lauren, Jason and Mark sent: a beautiful arrangement of white flowers in the shape of a cradle. Now Becky is leaning forward and throwing a white rose after Thomas' coffin. She whispers something Cathy can't hear, then she and Adam stand hunched together. What did it all mean, a baby being born and dying two days later? Cathy doesn't know. Maybe it means nothing. Maybe life is just a series of totally random events. And yet, it's hard for Cathy to feel that, when underneath all this sadness, is so much love and friendship.

Loving, really loving someone, is a special kind of power, isn't it? Cathy can feel it pulsing all around Adam and Becky now. Surely, nothing can wipe that out; not even death. It goes on, somehow.

Adam and Becky slowly lead the trail back to the cars and Becky's house, where her mum is putting on a light lunch. Her mum has taken over all the funeral arrangements. She and Mark now walk beside Adam and Becky, while behind them are Reuben and Adam's mother, Lauren and her mum – and Jason.

Jason turns back and sees Cathy, still staring at the grave. He touches her lightly on the shoulder. She turns round and can't help noticing how handsome he looks in his dark suit. Then, rather self-consciously, she points at the flowers all around the grave. 'Beautiful, aren't they?'

Jason doesn't say anything for a moment, then he says, 'I'm going to choose really happy songs for my funeral, just to annoy everyone, like *Yellow Submarine*.' He sounds angry but then, more gently, he says, 'Let's go, shall we?'

Cathy nods. 'Yes, I'm ready.'

They follow after the others, who are already getting into cars. Then, Cathy blinks in amazement. For a moment, she thinks she's dreaming. But then, Jason cries out, 'Hey, it's Jez.'

7

'I Don't Fancy
You Anymore'

The waitress hands Cathy and Jez hot towels. Jez
starts using his to wipe his neck. Cathy says, 'I love
these towels, they smell all hot and lemony. I'd like
to take them home with me.'

'Make your own,' says Jez. 'Just slip the towels
in the microwave for a few seconds and squirt some
lemonade on them.' The waitress returns with a
pot of jasmine tea. Jez is dabbing his face with the
towel now. He smiles up at the waitress. 'I thought
I may as well get cleaned up. I haven't washed for
about a month.' The waitress gives him a nervous
laugh and hastily exits.

'She thinks you're quite mad,' says Cathy. 'And
she's right.' Jez opens the lid of the teapot. 'What
are you doing?'

'I'm just checking there aren't any fish swimming
in here.'

'What!' cries Cathy, at once.

'It's an old Chinese custom to put a goldfish in your tea. It's supposed to bring you luck . . . Oh yeah, we've just the one in here.'

Cathy springs forward. 'But that's disgusting.' She glares down into the teapot, then back at Jez. An evil gleam is lighting up those sleepy-looking eyes. 'I don't know why I believe anything you tell me. I never will again.'

'Want to hear something really disgusting? That guy behind you is blowing his nose in the serviette.'

'Trust you to notice that,' says Cathy. 'Still, it was a lovely meal, I really enjoyed it. Thank you.'

'I enjoyed it too,' says Jez. 'In fact, tonight has been cosmic.'

'All right, sarky,' says Cathy.

'No truly,' says Jez. 'I haven't had so much excitement since I was born.' His eyes are gleaming with amusement again.

'I don't know why I speak to you,' laughs Cathy. They've spent most of the meal trading quips and amused glints. Then she gives a teasing smile. 'Took you long enough to ask me, though, didn't it? How many weeks have you been back – eight, nine?'

'But Cathy, I was terrified you'd turn me down. I'm a very sensitive person, you know.' He picks up his cup. 'Send the cups back – they haven't got any handles.'

'Ha, ha,' says Cathy.

'No, honestly, it's taken me weeks to pluck up courage to ask you out for this meal. I've been all day getting ready.'

'Really.' Cathy raises a sceptical eyebrow.

'Yeah, I put on my best trousers.'

Cathy starts to laugh.

'Why are you laughing?'

'Those trousers are disgusting.'

'Nothing wrong with my cream trousers.'

'They look like they've been made out of lampshade material, they're all weaved and your shirt hasn't been washed for about a century. You certainly haven't brushed your hair and you've got bits of food in your beard.' She's smiling as she says it. Yet, she can't help admitting, she'd felt more than a bit insulted that Jez had taken so little trouble over his appearance tonight. He could have brushed his hair, couldn't he?

'Are you saying I look a mess?'

'Yes.' They're both laughing and yet Cathy senses that neither of them's completely joking.

'That's the last time I take you out, then,' says Jez. 'You've blown it, which reminds me: that guy who blew his nose into the serviette is now holding hands with his girlfriend. Just thought you'd like to know.'

'I'm just gripped by that saga. Do keep me posted on further developments.'

110

There's silence for a moment. Jez looks just a tiny bit deflated. Surely her comments about his appearance can't have upset him? Tonight, any girl would have told him to sort it out.

'Jason's driving Lauren up to Birmingham for her interview tomorrow,' Cathy says, conversationally. 'And I've got a ten hour shift at the *Pizza Paradiso*, which I'm really looking forward to. And so's Becky, I don't think. How about you? Working on your building site, tomorrow?'

'Last day. They've offered me another two weeks but I'm not too pushed on physical graft. I just did it for the dosh, so I could give my mum a bit of rent and take you out so you could insult me.' He grins. 'Last night, my mum and dad cracked open the sherry and said they wanted to talk about my future. We had a nice, short chat. About twenty seconds. They asked if I had any career plans.'

'What did you say?'

'I said, just one: I was seriously thinking of taking up a career as a cat burglar – short hours, no taxes.'

'You'd never fit through the windows.'

'You're very cutting tonight. Anyway, my parents were none too happy about that one. I think my mum's still hoping I'm going to turn into a city gent. I'm sure she's got a bowler and an umbrella tucked away for me. I told her, the one thing I do really well is nothing. Most people have to keep busy. But not me.'

111

'There's always your sweet shop,' says Cathy.

He sighs nostalgically. 'Yeah, I often think about that. I'd have a room above the shop, down in the west country, three customers a day. I'd grow some veg and finish my novel.'

'You've started writing?'

'In my head. I've got so many books inside my head.'

'What are they about?'

'Things I've seen on my travels. Travel does change you, Cathy, opens you out. That's why everyone in Cartford's got the same opinions; they haven't seen anything. I'm getting itchy feet again, Cathy. Thought I might check out Italy next, see what's going on there.'

'But you can't go yet, you've only just come back.'

'I'm getting restless already, to tell the truth. What's Cartford got anyway: vandalised phone boxes and flashy burger bars. And after you've seen Berlin . . .'

'What's so great about Berlin, then?' interrupts Cathy, feeling suddenly defensive about Cartford.

'You haven't got all those bloody DIY shops everywhere, for a start. And it's not a tragedy if your neighbour's got the same door as you. The streets are so clean you wouldn't believe it, and when you go for a drink, you never have to stand up, because there are lots of places around the bar.

112

And there's just a better atmosphere – you'd have to see it really but there's none of the nastiness you get in pubs here, if you happen to catch the wrong guy's eye, you get beaten up. I hate and detest that. The Germans are more civilised. And they've got good bookshops. Admit it, Cathy, Cartford's a dump, isn't it?'

'It's got its faults, yes,' says Cathy. 'But it's still where we grew up, where our roots are – and all our friends. I could never push off and forget my friends.'

'I've never forgotten my friends,' says Jez, with unexpected force. 'I may not have written long letters,' he half-smiles, 'but often I'd be sitting on the Rhine – where unlike the Thames there aren't any bloody great buildings blocking your view – having a bottle or two of wine and thinking about Lauren and Jason, Mark, Becky and Adam, even you sometimes, and wondering what you were all doing. Sometimes I'd try and work out what time it was in merry old England, so then I could say, they'll be going down the pub now or ... yes ... I'll tell you something that's been on my mind for about five seconds. Next time, why don't you come with me? Think about it.' Then, before Cathy can reply, he's disappeared to pay the bill.

When he returns, to her great surprise, he bends over and kisses her smack on the lips; it's quite a long kiss too. Then he looks at her as if expecting

113

her to say something, as if, in fact, this was a first date. But it's not a date, it's just two very good friends out having a laugh together, isn't it? So Cathy's too stunned to say anything and Jez immediately acts as if it never happened.

'Jason, I've really got to work now.' Lauren says it as sweetly as she can but her foot is tapping impatiently against her desk.

Jason remains sprawled across her bed. Then he says, 'You don't want to be doing that.'

'Yes, I do, Jason, and I've got to do it tonight because tomorrow I've got my interview and it's already a week late. The whole file's got to be finished by next month.'

Jason yawns. 'I don't know how you can do all that crap. Personally, I'd rather be fed to sharks.' He winks. 'Don't be depressed, let me buy you a drink.'

'Jason, I can't.' Lauren can feel herself getting more and more stressed. Why won't he go? At first when he used to come round every night, Lauren liked it. In fact, she encouraged it. She even used to invite him round on nights when she knew he had sports training, just as a little test, to see how serious he was. So now, he never plays any sport. In fact, he doesn't really do anything much, except see her. And it's too much, she needs some spare time to herself. And some time to work.

114

'Look, Jason, this essay is part of my A level assessment,' her tone sharpens. 'You should be encouraging me anyway, not being negative.'

'Who's being negative? You work, I won't say a word, honestly.'

Lauren takes up her pen.

'I wonder how Cathy and Jez are getting on?' asks Jason, suddenly. Lauren glares at him. 'Sorry, sorry, won't say another word. I promise.' He sits up. 'I'll watch you work.'

Lauren copies out the essay-title. She turns round to see Jason staring at her. 'Oh no, don't watch me . . . it's no good Jason, you've got to go.'

'What have I done now?'

'Nothing, it's just . . .' Her bedroom door bursts open and her dad is suddenly glowering in front of them. He strides over to Jason, grabs hold of his shirt collar and pulls him to his feet. Then he roars, 'When my daughter's studying for her exams, you are banned from this house.' He starts jabbing Jason's neck with his fingers. 'Banned, do you understand?'

Jason doesn't reply. He doesn't even seem to have heard what her father's said. He just stares fixedly ahead of him. Lauren remembers Jason doing this at school. Whenever a teacher had a go at him, Jason would just stare over their heads, as if they were some lower form of life whose existence he didn't even acknowledge.

Then, Jason starts brushing his collar down, with what teachers used to call 'an insolent smile' on his face. He strolls to the door. Lauren calls out his name but he doesn't look back. Lauren springs to her feet. Her dad places himself in front of her, still breathing heavily. 'Let him go.'

'No,' she cries, but then she hears the front door slam shut. 'You had no right to do that.'

'I had every right. If you're not careful, you're going to fail all your exams.'

'I know. But Jason's helping, he's driving me for my interview tomorrow, you know.'

'He's a waste of space, that lad. Nothing but a glorified shop-assistant – and that's all he'll ever be. Well, that's fine, but I'm not having him drag you down too. And that's what he's doing, dragging you down. The nights you have homework you stay in on your own and do it. Right?' Now he's jabbing a finger at her.

'Oh yes, plan my whole life for me, why don't you,' Lauren snaps, glaring at her father.

'That's it. No more,' he says. She doesn't push it. He can stay in a bad mood for days sometimes.

He thumps to the door, then says, 'You'll thank me for this one day . . . and I mean what I say, that lad is banned on weekdays.'

Lauren slumps back in front of her desk. She feels more trapped than ever. She wanted Jason to go but not like that. Now her dad's in a mood –

and Jason . . . Should she ring him up and apologise? Yes, she will and then she'll end up talking to him for hours. That's why she must start her essay now. She stares down at the title: 'Discuss the relationship between Mr and Mrs Morel in *Sons and Lovers*', but all she can think about is the relationship between her and Jason. Maybe she should ring him now. But then she hears the telephone downstairs. She rushes to the stairs and hears her father say, 'At the moment, Lauren is doing her homework. I suggest you . . .'

But his suggestion is lost to the air as Lauren snatches the receiver from him. 'Hello,' she cries.

'Lauren, it's Russell.'

'Oh, hello Russell,' she tries to hide the disappointment in her voice.

'I just rang up to wish you good luck.'

'That's nice of you.'

'I know. So what time's the interview?'

'Two o'clock.'

'You going by train, then, are you?'

'No, Jason's driving me.'

There's a pause. 'I'm sure his teeth will shine.'

'What's that supposed to mean?' asks Lauren, immediately defensive.

'Nothing.'

'No, tell me.'

'Well, come on Lauren, you've got to admit, he loves himself. You've only got to see him strutting

117

through the town with one hand in his jeans pocket.'

'A bit, maybe,' concedes Lauren, 'but he loves himself with taste.'

'I don't agree. Everything about that guy's image winds me up, actually. But I can see how a certain type of girl would like him. But not you.'

'Really.'

'Yeah, you're different. I see you with someone a bit . . .'

'Like you,' prompts Lauren.

Russell laughs. 'Yeah.' Lauren laughs too. Russell's such a fan of hers. It's flattering and just a bit dangerous. 'Damian and I were wondering when you were going to invite us round.'

Lauren laughs again. 'Don't hold your breath.'

'You're cruel,' says Russell.

'I know . . . and now I've got to do that *Sons and Lovers* essay.'

'I finished it last week.'

'Don't.'

'Let us know how you get on, won't you?'

'I will. Bye.' Lauren smiles to herself for a moment. Russell always cheers her up. Maybe she will invite him and Damian around one evening. Maybe!

Back upstairs, she slumps in front of her essay-title. All she can think about is Jason. Her father really was out of order chucking Jason out like that.

She wonders where he's gone. Is he sitting in a pub somewhere pouring out his woes to some girl? She bristles. It's then she hears a tap on her window. She jumps up and peers outside. Nothing! She sits down again.

Then, she hears another tap. Someone is throwing stones against her window. She opens her window a little, 'Jason,' she whispers, 'Jason.' And at once he appears from behind the bush. It's at that moment too that the moon bobs out from the cloud and she sees him, grinning all over his face. It's funny how young he looks when he smiles. It's as if beneath the 'I'm so hard' mask is nothing but a big kid.

Now he's beckoning at her to come down. Lauren shakes her head. 'I've got to work,' she mouths. But he just beckons at her more insistently, then he flashes another of his smiles at her. And she thinks – oh, what the hell. She's not going to do any more work tonight.

So she tiptoes down the stairs, clicks the door gently behind her and rushes towards the silvery darkness – and Jason.

'Anyway, I'd better let you go.' He looks at his watch. 'Oh, my goodness, yes. We're already twenty minutes over time. Sorry.'

Lauren smiles at Sean Kobal, her interviewer. 'I've enjoyed it,' she says. And, to her surprise, she has enjoyed it. They started by talking about books but then they moved on to plays and films; it was all very relaxed, really.

Perhaps because Sean is much younger than she'd expected, brown hair in a pony-tail, fresh-faced, a ready grin and so enthusiastic about everything. Also, he really listened to everything Lauren said, or he seemed to, anyhow.

'I can't say anything officially, but . . .' he smiles, 'I think I can say you'll be hearing from us.'

'That's excellent. Thank you, thank you,' gushes Lauren.

He gets up. 'I'll let you get back now. Where have you come from – Cartford. Quite a journey home then, isn't it?'

'It's been worth it,' says Lauren.

He walks to the door with her. 'I expect life is pretty intense at the moment, with all the course-work due in any day now?'

'Yes, that's right,' says Lauren, with a thud of guilt. She's weeks behind now. In fact, she's beginning to wonder if she'll ever catch up.

'I'll see you out. You need a map to get out of here, don't you,' he says.

'When I was shown down here, I felt as if I was a contestant on *The Crystal Maze*,' says Lauren.

He laughs. '*The Crystal Maze*, that's a wild programme, isn't it?' And then they're off talking about *The Rocky Horror Show* as he guides her up

120

two flights of steps and down another maze of rooms, some of which have small queues of students waiting outside. That'll be me in a few months' time, thinks Lauren, with a tremor of excitement.

Now they are out in the reception area again. He stops walking but carries on telling her about a production of *The Rocky Horror Show* he saw last year. And it's then she hears her name being called, loudly, insistently. Somehow, Lauren had assumed Jason would be waiting for her outside in the car. But instead, he's lying sprawled across two chairs in reception, with his headphones on and a cigarette dangling out of his mouth. Just above his head is, of course, a NO SMOKING sign. It's a typically flashy Jason pose. And a few years ago Lauren might have been impressed. But not now, not here.

Now, he just looks like a yob. 'Lauren,' he calls again, so loudly that this time Sean looks across too. Lauren can feel herself bursting into technicolour. 'That's my friend . . . he drove me here.'

'Ah, I see,' says Sean. His eye catches Jason's. Jason stares back at him, as if he were some guy in a pub he'd caught eyeing Lauren up.

'You kept her a long time,' Jason says, accusingly. Sean ignores this.

'I won't keep you then, Lauren.' She can almost hear the friendliness draining out of his voice.

'Bye, thanks so much,' she calls after him. She

121

turns to Jason. There's so much anger and frustration flaming inside her that for a split second, she can't speak at all.

'What . . . Why did you do that?'

'Do what?' drawls Jason.

She starts pushing his boots on to the ground. 'The way you're sitting like that.' Jason lowers his feet on to the carpet. 'And you were so rude to him – my interviewer. He's the guy who decides if I get offered a place here or not. And he was being so nice to me.'

'You can see why,' mutters Jason. 'He fancies you.'

'Is that what you think?'

'Yes. And you were flirting round him. Got a thing about lecturers, haven't you?'

'How dare you!' cries Lauren. 'How dare you!' she repeats. 'You're always against me, aren't you, whatever I do. You don't want me to succeed, do you?' She's almost screaming at him, while Jason's voice is low and oddly distant, as if it's coming from deep inside him.

'I drove you here, didn't I, even though . . .' He stops.

'Even though what? Come on, let's have it.'

Jason's voice is barely above a whisper now. 'You're just holding on to me until you've got your exams. Then, you'll go to university and forget all

122

about me. You're using me. You're bloody selfish, Lauren.'

Lauren stares hard at him. 'No, I'm not,' she says quickly. Actually, a few times recently she had wondered what would happen to them when she went to university. But she'd deliberately blocked it out. She'd think about that later. There were enough things to worry about right now.

'We could still see each other. You could drive up for weekends,' she adds, rather weakly. Then her anger flares up again. 'Still, if you have your way, I'll fail all my exams, won't I? That's what you'd like, isn't it?' Her head's drumming with anger now. 'Me stuck in Cartford all my life, ending up like you – a shop-assistant.'

Immediately, she wishes she hadn't said that. She hadn't meant to. There's a brief and rather unpleasant pause. Jason gets to his feet. 'You can make your own way home,' he announces, and strides away.

She's too stunned even to reply. Should she run after him and apologise? No, because this was his fault, really. He had no right to act like that in front of her interviewer. He started it. Instead, she slumps down in her chair. He'll be back in a minute. He can't really leave her here. But she shouldn't have made that crack about him being a shop-assistant. That really hurt him, didn't it?

Then she feels angry with herself for feeling guilty. How often must she tell herself: this isn't her fault.

After a few minutes she can wait no longer. She'll walk back to the car, where Jason will, of course, be waiting. But when she gets outside, she sees with a gasp of horror that the car really has gone. She was so convinced he'd be sitting in the car, staring into space. And instead, well, he's definitely in the wrong now, isn't he? For a moment this thought cheers her.

Then she just feels very tired and weary. She'll have to ring home, explain it to her dad. Unless she rings Cathy. Yes, she'll ring Cathy. But she remembers that Cathy has just started working at the *Pizza Paradiso* now. She could ring her at work, of course. But what a mess! What a total mess!

It's then she sees a familiar car tear into the reception area at about a thousand miles-an-hour. The car screeches to a stop in front of her. Lauren could almost weep with relief. Thank goodness Jason has come back. But she doesn't move. In fact, she doesn't even acknowledge his presence. She just stares stonily ahead. The car door flies open. Jason gets out and leans against the car.

'Want a lift?' he says, lightly.

Lauren turns on him. 'I don't believe you,' she cries. 'Just leaving me because . . . Where did you go? Oh, I don't care where you went. I was just going to ring Cathy, you know. You're . . .'

'Mad,' prompts Jason.

'Yes, sometimes I think you are.'

'My parents think I'm mad too, they've given up on me. It runs in our family. It's in the genes. I've got two cousins who are off their heads and an uncle . . .'

'Oh, I don't care about your uncle. This is happening too often,' she says and slips inside the car.

He slides in beside her. And even while she's angry with him, Lauren can't help noticing how easily, effortlessly he moves, like a dancer.

'Take you home?' he says.

'Yes,' she snaps.

They don't talk the whole way home. Jason just keeps switching the music up louder and louder. By the time they reach Cartford it's deafening.

Becky taps on the door, then opens it. Inside, Mark is sitting behind a desk. As soon as he sees Becky he springs to his feet. 'This is a surprise,' he cries.

'I've been meaning to pop in for ages,' she says.

'It's just a box-room really.' Mark waves around at his desk, the filing cabinet and chairs. Then he points to the telephone. 'Still, it's good to have my own telephone. Have to keep this room locked, so no one else uses it. Coffee?' he adds, flicking on the kettle beside him.

Becky nods and sits down. 'But this is so good. Your own office.'

'It's not completely mine. The other execs. can use it too but it's all right, isn't it?'

'You've done so well.'

'You reckon?' Mark beams. 'I'm getting there but everything takes so much longer than I thought.'

'I see they're painting the student union.'

'Yeah. You'd be surprised how long it takes to get permission just to buy some paint. There are so many people afraid to say, "Yes". They're painting out all the graffiti as I'm going to have a special board for graffiti, that's the plan anyway. Did you know we did a sleep-out for charity on Friday?'

'No. How did that go?'

Mark reaches for two cups and puts a spoonful of coffee in each. 'Pretty good, apart from the fact a load of food I'd left in the the tent got stolen. And about three in the morning it just bucketed down. When I woke up I didn't know what was happening. I had this stereo pounding away in my ears, rain dripping down my face.'

Becky laughs. 'So what did you do?'

'Luckily, the caretaker had left me the keys to the changing room so we all legged it in there. I managed to get a place right next to the heater. It was a laugh, though. Only powdered milk, I'm afraid.'

'That's okay.'

'Got my first offer from Brighton today, two Cs.

I might get that, if I'm lucky. Did you hear Lauren got offered two Bs from Birmingham?'

'Yeah, and she was really worried about that, because Jason was rude to one of her lecturers. They had an almighty row about that, didn't they?'

'So what's new?' says Mark airily. 'They're always rowing about something these days. I expect Cathy's been playing the peace-maker as usual.' Mark plonks Becky's coffee down in front of her. 'So what's it like being back in college again?'

'Weird. I've been away so long now. For some reason, I keep remembering my first day here, you know, when I got lost and stumbled into the hall, late. I was so relieved when you waved me over.' Mark grins. 'And then we went for a wander around and I was really impressed that you'd even got one of those college handouts for me.'

'It seems ages ago now, doesn't it?' says Mark. But he can remember every detail of that day, even down to the dappy green trainers Becky wore. Today, on each wrist, she's wearing a gold jangly bracelet, just like she used to. He feels a rush of longing for Becky, as she was then. Before she left him so far behind.

'How's Adam?' he asks, conversationally. 'I've been meaning to give him a bell.'

'That's partly why I'm here. I've got a bit of news about Adam and me,' she looks nervous. 'We're going to get married.'

'You are?' gasps Mark. 'So when was this decided?'

'I don't know exactly. We've talked about it a lot lately.'

'Adam didn't get down on one knee, then?'

'No, nothing like that.' A smile flickers across her face. 'We just thought . . . well, we'd planned to get married before, and we both still want to. We've fixed a day, September 20th to be precise, as that gives us a little time to arrange things, and it's just after my birthday and everyone will still be around.' She looks at Mark anxiously.

'So,' he says, 'congratulations.'

'I know we're quite young.'

'Yes, you are.' Mark stares at her, feeling the old familiar stab of jealousy. Only it seems further away, just an echo really. Is he getting over Becky at last? It's about time. 'But you and Adam, you've never left the fast lane, have you? I haven't got off the starting post and yet you've finished already. I don't mean finished,' he corrects himself hastily, 'you know.'

'Yes.' They both become self-conscious. 'Apart from my mum, you're the very first to know,' says Becky. 'You are just a little bit pleased, aren't you? I know it sounds as if we're rushing things.'

'No, not really. You spend so much time together already . . .' there's a hint of bitterness in his voice

128

as he says this, 'you must know each other really well.'

'Yes, we do. The funny thing is, you don't know how much of yourself there is until someone else wants to know.' She pauses, 'I couldn't have got through these last months without Adam and he said – well, he said the same. Just before I came here I told Thomas about the wedding. I often go up and tell him things. It helps me sort things out in my mind. You probably think I'm mad.'

'No, I don't,' says Mark. But he does feel awkward whenever Becky mentions Thomas. 'So anyway, do you know where you're going to live yet?'

'Yes. For now, Mum and I are going to swap rooms. She's going to make her room into a kind of flat for us. It'll just be a registry office wedding, a little reception for a few close friends.'

'The Inner Circle.'

'Exactly. And we'd be really pleased if you'd be Adam's best man.'

'That'd be an honour,' says Mark.

'Oh good.' Becky flushes with excitement. 'I'm so happy about this and I did want you to be happy too.'

'I am,' says Mark, firmly. 'By the way, what exactly does a best man do?'

'Why don't you come round one night and we'll tell you all the gory details.'

'All right.'

'I can cook you a meal, if you like. Neither Adam nor I are working next Thursday evening, if that's any good.'

'I'll just check the old diary.'

'Such a busy man.'

'Oh yeah, let's see, yes, Thursday next week will be great.'

The door opens and two girls chorus, 'Mark, we've finished. Do come and have a look.'

'Okay, I won't be a minute. You didn't let Julie paint lips and flowers all over the wall, did you?'

'You'll have to see, won't you.' Then, one of the girls notices Becky. 'Oh, hi Becky, how are you?'

'I'm fine. And you?'

'We're all right,' says the girl. 'Still at the *Pizza Paradiso*, then?'

'Yes, still there. In fact, I'll be there in about an hour's time. But I'm planning to come back to college in the autumn, do a few evening classes.'

'That's nice.' The girl turns back to Mark. 'Hurry up then, Mark.' Then they both giggle and exit.

'I dread to think what they've done,' says Mark.

Becky gets up. 'I'd better go.' Then she adds unexpectedly, 'I never thought I'd marry this young, you know. And even after I met Adam . . . it's so gradual at first. It just crept up on me, until suddenly I couldn't imagine a day without him. But if Adam is the one, and he is, why wait.'

Mark gets up. All the time they've been talking there's been a desk between them. He catches her by the arm, just as she's opening the door. 'You and Adam, you're like Laurel and Hardy, really, aren't you? A double-act for all time.'

She turns round and takes his arm. 'Yes, that's it, exactly.' And Mark can't miss the excited break in her voice. 'Thank you Mark. You know you're the best friend I've ever had.'

Lauren is serving up the stew which her mother has left her for dinner, when the doorbell rings. Who's that? At least it won't be Jason, as he's gone to the cinema with Jez tonight. She's quite shocked at how relieved she is about that. Perhaps it's because, every time she sees Jason, it's so tense; there are just so many undercurrents now. No wonder she can never concentrate on her home-work.

She opens the door to see Russell smiling rather nervously at her. 'So this is where you live,' he says. Lauren releases a slow smile. 'Is this a bad moment? he asks.

'For what?'

'That book on D. H. Lawrence you were going to lend me.' There's a glint in his eye now as if he knows what a pathetic excuse this is. 'I haven't disturbed you, have I?'

'I was just eating.' Now there's a gleam in Lauren's eye too. 'Have you eaten?'

'No, I haven't, actually. Is there enough for two?'

'My mum's left me enough for ten. She thinks I need feeding up . . . come in.'

He follows her into the hall. 'Amazing house you've got here. How many rooms have you got? A thousand?'

'About that.'

She takes him into the kitchen; he sniffs and says, 'Smells all right . . .' Then he asks, 'All on your own tonight?'

'Yes, my parents have gone to a dinner and dance.'

'And what about Mr Image?'

'He's gone to see the new Arnold Schwarzenegger film – and don't call him that. You don't really know him at all.' In her head, Lauren has been slagging Jason off a lot lately, but it still irritates her when an outsider does it.

'I'm sorry, he's obviously more intelligent than he looks.'

Lauren wishes she hadn't invited Russell in now. He's beginning to irritate her, actually, lording it there, in his very squeaky leather jacket and designer shirt, which screams, 'Notice Me'. And

132

so what if Jason's not doing A levels. That doesn't mean he's not too hot on brain cells. Far from it.

She flings some cutlery down on the table. Picking up the change in temperature, Russell, says, 'I won't overstay my welcome.'

'No, you won't,' replies Lauren.

'You've had your hair done, haven't you? Looks good.' Lauren smiles to herself. He's back playing her humble admirer. 'I'm about ready to serve,' she says. It's then the doorbell rings again. 'I don't believe it,' she says.

'Actually,' says Russell, 'I think I know who that is. It's Damian. He said he might drop in to see if I actually came round.'

'Is this a dare or something, then?'

'No, not exactly. But you know Damian, has to see what's going on.' The doorbell rings again. 'Just tell him I'm here, having dinner with you. There's no need to ask him in.'

Lauren, highly amused by all this, goes to the door with a smile on her face. But as soon as she opens the door, the smile vanishes. For Jason and Jez are framed in the doorway.

'Couldn't get in,' says Jason. 'Sold out when we arrived.'

Lauren can only gape at them. This is a nightmare. When Jason walks in and sees Russell sitting at the kitchen table, he'll go ape. But how can she stop him walking in?

133

Lauren is about to tell them that she's working when Jez declares, 'I can smell food. I'm starving.'

'Going to invite us in, then?' asks Jason. His tone is challenging, almost aggressive. She hates the way he assumes he can wander into her house whenever he likes.

They're inside now and as they walk to the kitchen, Lauren mentions, as casually as she can, 'Oh yes, Russell dropped in to borrow a book and he's staying for dinner, too.'

Jason doesn't say anything but the tension is unbearable. Lauren's heart gives a thump as she introduces Russell to Jez. 'And you know Jason,' she says.

'Yes, we've met,' says Russell. 'All right, lads,' he says. Jason gives a contemptuous laugh in reply. Then Russell's gaze turns back to Jez and he gives a rather sneery smile. Lauren hates Russell for doing that.

Jez falls into a chair, while Jason, dressed all in black, hovers menacingly in the doorway. He looks as if he's waiting to attack someone. Lauren puts out some plates, then turns to Jez. Thank goodness he's here. 'Cathy was saying you haven't been feeling too well.'

'Yeah, I keep feeling as if I'm going to collapse.' Jez chuckles, as if he's said something funny.

'Cathy says you're drinking too much.'

'It could be drinking, could be smoking, could

134

be just food . . . I dropped in on the doc yesterday. He thought it might be stress brought on by over-work.' Jez laughs again. This time, Lauren joins in. Jez continues, 'Cathy's trying to get me to give up smoking. Yesterday, I let her throw all my cig-gies out. Of course, at one o'clock this morning, I'm out rooting through all the bins desperate for one. But don't tell Cathy. She also reckons I should take up jogging.'

'That I must see,' says Lauren. 'You must take photographs.' She starts to relax. Then her eyes turn to Jason, doing his impression of an assassin, waiting to strike.

After Russell's gone, she and Jason are going to have an almighty row about this. Another one. 'Are you joining us?' she asks Jason. Her voice is cool, slightly mocking. He gives another laugh, which isn't really a laugh and slides on to a chair.

'You're not at college, are you?' Russell asks Jez.

'No,' says Jez.

'So what do you do?' asks Russell.

Lauren laughs as she doles the stew on to plates. 'Now, there's a question.'

'I'm what you might call semi-retired. I am sell-ing tickets and tapes for this rockabilly band called, "The Tree Cutters", who no one has heard of, so it doesn't take up too much time.'

'There you go, Russell,' Lauren says, putting the plate down beside him. And it's then Jason lets out this great howl of anger and slams his fist on to the table. Lauren gives a terrified gasp.

'You served him first,' yells Jason. Then he slams his fist on to the table again. 'Why?'

The question roars around the room. Lauren glares at him, while swelling up inside her she can feel such anger and frustration. How dare he act like this. How dare he.

'Can I have a word with you outside, now please?'

'Yeah, sure,' he cries, springing to his feet.

Lauren marches to the front door and hurls it open. 'I want you to go home now,' she announces.

'Don't be silly.'

'I mean it, Jason. Just go, will you.'

He beams his eyes on to her, 'I'm sorry,' he whispers. How often has he said that and how often has Lauren given him another chance. 'I was well out of order, wasn't I?'

'Yes.'

'I've got to give you a bit more freedom, I know. I will try.'

'But you can't do it,' says Lauren.

'Yes I can. I'm truly, truly sorry,' he adds.

'No, you'll never change. And it just goes on getting worse and worse. Now, it's over.' The harshness in her voice shocks even her, while Jason is visibly flinching.

'What are you saying?' his voice is suddenly hoarse.

'I'm saying, I don't want you to come round any more because it's so intense all the time. I can't stand it. I feel you never leave me any time for myself. You want everything from me.'

There's silence for a moment, as Lauren's fingers clutch the door handle even more tightly, while Jason looms in front of her, his face a mask, except for those eyes; they're pleading with her, begging her. 'We can't finish like this,' he says. 'Not us.'

For a moment his words jolt her. But then she thinks again of these last weeks. She says, 'We finished some weeks ago, actually. Since then, it's been sheer torture. We're just dragging each other down. It's better for both of us this way.'

She falters. Jason is looking so bewildered, so helpless. For a moment she feels a pang of sadness. She's all he's got, really. Deep down, he's a lonely person. And he'd do anything for her. But then he declares, 'It's him in there, isn't it? That geek you've been seeing behind my back. I knew this would happen. I even had dreams about it.'

'Think that if you like,' says Lauren, wearily. 'To be honest, I don't care any more.' Then she adds flatly, 'It's over.' He doesn't move. Why won't he go? She screams, 'I don't fancy you any more, all right.'

Then he comes to life, rushing past her, without another word. For a second, she breathes in his familiar, clean smell and then he's outside, standing by his car yelling, 'Once I walk away, I never come back.' He hesitates, looks back at her. But Lauren says nothing.

She watches him get into his car and tear away. Jason was incapable of leaving her house quietly. It was always a noisy ceremony. But now, he's gone for good. He'll never drive up to her house again. It really is over.

She should go back to the others. But her feet are nailed to the ground, unable to leave the scene of the crime. Crime? She hasn't done anything wrong. What has she done?

She hadn't meant to finish with him tonight. Not at all. It was only that when he banged his fist on the table and started shouting, he really scared her. And then all these feelings that had been inside her – for weeks really – just burst out.

From what seems like far away, she can hear Russell's voice. 'Do you want me to go?' It's quite a shock to turn round and see him just behind her shoulder.

'Would you mind? It's just . . .'

'I understand.' He seems keen to go. 'I'll pick up the book tomorrow.'

'Oh, no, let me get it for you,' she cries. She walks slowly forward, her legs still feeling alarmingly heavy. 'It's upstairs.' Then she sees Jez, looking awkward. 'Shall I push off, too?' he asks.

She grasps his hand. 'No, no, please stay, I won't be a moment. I'm just getting a book for,' for a moment she forgets his name, 'Russell.' She feels so strange, all disorientated, as if she were very drunk. She stumbles on to her bed, totally forgetting why she's there. Then she shivers violently. That scene with Jason was so horrible. But it had to be done, hadn't it?

It hits her again; she's finished with Jason. The only boy she's ever loved. But now she's free to be herself. That's what she wanted. She's done the right thing, hasn't she? But no one answers.

8

'I Want You to Come With Me'

'I thought you might like to take a peek at your future residence,' says Becky's mum to Adam as she waves around her room. 'In the summer, I'm going to have this room transformed into a mini-flat. You'll have a television, radio and cassette player – and a kettle. I'm not trying to keep you up here, you understand,' she says. 'Use downstairs whenever, but I want you to feel independent; and by the way, do call me Margaret.'

Adam is quite overwhelmed by all this generosity. 'This is very good of you,' he says. And it is. That's why he feels particularly mean that he's not more excited by it all. He was at first. But now it's sinking in, that all he's doing really is moving out of his house to stay with Becky's mum. And however nice she is – and she is really nice – he will still be a guest in someone else's house. There's no way he could just come in and raid the fridge or something.

Now he's being ungrateful. Would he rather be living in digs with Becky? In a way, he would. Then he hears Becky coming up the stairs. 'That was Mark,' she says breathlessly. 'Something's happened: Jason and Lauren have split up.'

'Since when?' asks Adam

'Since last night,' says Becky. 'Jason's at Mark's now.'

'So Mark's not coming round,' says Becky's mum.

'Yes he is, because Jason's going out in a few minutes on a date with a model . . . but Mark'll be about half-an-hour late.'

'I see, so I'd better go and switch everything down,' says Becky's mum.

After she's gone, Adam asks, 'So tell, what's happened? Has Jason been doing the dirty on Lauren, then?'

'No, not at all. Jason thinks Lauren's been seeing Russell behind his back. Lauren denies it. I know they'd had quite a few rows, but still it's a shock. They belong together. Jez was there when it happened and Cathy knows. It shakes you up, doesn't it, when people break up?' There's a silence. The news has unnerved them both.

Finally, Adam says, 'I think the hardest thing in this planet is trusting people, really trusting them.

And that's what I reckon went wrong with Jason and Lauren; they never trusted each other.'

'While we . . . ' prompts Becky.

'Yes, I think we do trust each other.' Adam sits down on her bed. 'I'll be honest though. When we first started going out, I'd think of you at college and then I'd picture the blokes you'd be meeting and all this anger would flare up inside me. And when I saw you I'd long to ask you which blokes you'd met today and if you liked any of them. Actually I did ask you.'

'When?'

'Many times. I'd sit in front of my mirror and have a right go at you. I'd question you for hours, usually in a heavy Scottish accent. Don't ask me why.'

Becky sighs. 'Snap. Only I never used a mirror. But in my head, I've had so many imaginary conversations with you. Often, late at night. That's when you'd tell me we were breaking up, that you'd met someone else. And then, after we lost Thomas and for a few days . . .'

'I lost myself,' interrupts Adam. 'It was as if I was in a kind of limbo. I just didn't want to go any further.' He puts his arms around Becky and begins to cover her face with kisses. Then he says, 'Jason and Lauren, they will get back together.'

Cathy hears the dogs first. Their barking grows

considerably louder as her car crunches up the driveway.

She steps outside. Once this was a farm. Now it's the animal rescue centre. Round the back, in great big runs, are animals which have been rescued from being bred for meat. There are rabbits the size of cats, and great big white chickens. There's also a mad women-hating goat with massive horns. Stray dogs are there too although well over twenty dogs and cats live inside the old farmhouse. And by the sound of it, they are all yapping excitedly at the door.

Neil, the son of the woman who runs the rescue centre, opens the door. Immediately, dogs are tearing around Cathy, who feels obliged to pat them all. 'Hello, yes, hello to you too and I haven't forgotten you, yes, you like to chew my finger, don't you?'

'Cup of tea, Cathy?' asks Neil.

Cathy hesitates. Last time she was here, she had tried making some toast but found it impossible to find any butter which didn't have cats' hairs on it. As if reading her thoughts, Neil says, 'It's all right, I've just washed the mugs.'

Neil is around Cathy's age, with black spiky hair and three rings on his nose, one either side and one in the middle. Cathy's fascinated by these rings. She even flirted with the idea of having them herself. The last time she came round – she's

143

becoming something of a regular here lately – she asked Neil if having the rings fitted on to his nose hurt. 'No, it just makes your eyes water for a few moments,' he said. But that was enough to put Cathy off.

'Okay, a cup of tea will be great. Then, I'll do some feeding,' says Cathy. This is how Cathy helps here.

'You just need to do the dogs and cats today,' says Neil. 'Jason's doing all the animals outside.'

'Jason?' Right away, Cathy's heart starts hammering.

'Yeah, he came round last night, stayed over. I'll go and see if he wants some tea. Make yourself at home. Mum's out at a demo but she should be back soon.'

Cathy goes into the lounge and sits down gingerly on one of the two sofas. Last time she sat here, she got flea-bites all up her arm. The place is just crawling with fleas. The dogs are still romping around her; one of them, a very old spaniel whose fur reeks, jumps up on the sofa beside her and starts licking her chin. Cathy strokes him, somewhat absent-mindedly. Jason's here. She just can't stop saying that to herself. And each time, she feels the same choking excitement.

When she lived with Lauren, she saw Jason every day. It was Lauren he'd come to see, not her, but he cast such a glow that she could steal a little of it. Since he and Lauren broke up – over two months ago now – Cathy's hardly seen him and she's missed him more than she can say. She did pop into his sports shop a couple of times and he was quite friendly, yet different somehow. Probably he thought she was on Lauren's side, but really, she wasn't.

In fact, she had a go at Lauren about the break-up. 'You can't finish with Jason over something so petty,' she'd said. Then Lauren had cried, 'Cathy, that was just the final straw. Why won't you under-stand that?' Cathy never mentioned it again. Ever since she and Lauren haven't been quite so close. And Cathy couldn't stop thinking about Jason and what he must be feeling. He'd made Lauren his life, so now he must be so lonely. And he must long to talk to someone; to Cathy. In the past he had confided in her. Surely he will again.

She could picture the scene so clearly. All her family – and Giles – will be in bed, when there's a mad knocking on the door. And there he'll be, looking both vulnerable and aggressive, as only he can; 'Cathy, have you got a minute?' Then he'll come in and talk and talk and talk. He'll tell her exactly how he feels about Lauren and his life . . . He'll tell Cathy everything, while Cathy is wise and sympathetic – her speciality. He'll stay for hours. Sometimes they'll talk all night, then they'll go for

145

a walk, just as the dawn rises. And it was so real, so clear. It had to happen.

Then she hears, 'Won't be a second with your tea, Jason. By the way, Cathy's here.'

She's spoken to him so often in her head lately, it's quite a jolt to see him in the flesh, with a dog in his arms and all the other dogs barking for attention. The dog in his arms is a whippet, nick-named 'Tripod' because he's only got three legs. Jason grins at Cathy, then sprawls out on the other sofa. She feels such a rush of affection for him, it scares her.

'This is a surprise,' she says.

He grins again. 'Yeah,' friendly but distant, keeping her at arm's length.

'I hardly see you these days,' she says. 'I've heard about you though, out with all your women.'

He just laughs. Come on, talk to me Jason, don't shut me out. Then she says, 'Haven't seen you here before.'

'No, shot over last night.'

'And he slept in Kelly's place,' says Neil, coming in with two mugs of tea.

'That's right,' says Jason, 'I crashed out on the sofa and woke up to hear this dog howling.' He laughs softly. 'In the end, he let Tripod and me share the sofa with him.'

'That Tripod,' says Neil, 'he steals all the other dogs' food.'

146

'Yeah, he's the toughest of them all, aren't you, Tripod?' says Jason proudly. Jason's dressed very casually in jeans with rips in them yet, somehow, he still looks smart. And he seems so relaxed and easy. But that's just a front. Cathy knows that. And he doesn't need to pretend with her. They're friends, close friends. He used to tell her things before. As soon as Neil disappears, Cathy says, 'I've missed you, you know.'

Jason catches her smile and smiles back. 'I nearly rang you a couple of times.'

'You should have.'

'I thought you'd be revising.'

'Don't. I should be revising now. But I needed to get away for a while . . . you know.'

Jason nods. 'I could never spend all that time sitting in.'

'Are you going out tonight?'

'Yeah, probably go clubbing it again tonight.'

Cathy feels a pang of disappointment. If he hadn't been going out she was going to suggest . . . she wasn't quite sure. But of course, he's going out. 'Who are you going out with?' she asks.

'Suzanne.'

'Oh.'

'She's a model,' adds Jason.

Is that information for Lauren's benefit? Suddenly, Cathy feels terribly depressed. 'We all seem to be going our own way these days, don't we? I mean, Mark's always doing college things and since I gave up working at the *Pizza Paradiso*, I hardly see Adam or Becky. Jez I do see, I've been helping him give up smoking. But this week he's been away with this band. And as for Lauren.' Jason immediately turns away. 'Lauren's always busy,' she says quickly.

'Not as busy as me,' snaps Jason. 'Most nights I'm out somewhere.'

'You want to be careful you don't burn yourself out,' says Cathy.

He gets up. 'Live fast, die young, have a good-looking corpse – that's me.'

That's one of Jason's favourite phrases. Or it was. He often said how the day he turned thirty he'd have a poison capsule waiting by his razor. 'Go out while you're still at the top,' he said. She remembers something else. Ages ago now, they certainly weren't more than eleven, they had to write an essay, set in the countryside. She's never forgotten what Jason wrote. His whole essay was, *The Boy Walked into the Duck Pond and Never Surfaced*. At the time, she thought that was pretty clever.

'You'll outlive us all,' she says, lightly.

Jason unexpectedly sits down again. 'No way,' he says firmly. 'When the party's over, I'll know to go.'

'But the party's hardly started yet.'

Jason doesn't seem to have heard her. 'I've got it all planned, you know. Have you seen the film *Quadrophenia*?'

'No.'

'It's about this guy who's a mod, has a blast for a while and then decides nothing's worth it and rather than dwindle away to nothing, he drives himself and his motorbike over a cliff... That's the way I'll do it.' Jason's such a showman, he's always saying things for effect. He likes to be dramatic. Cathy refuses to be impressed.

She says, 'One problem – there are no cliffs in Cartford.'

Jason doesn't smile, just says, flatly, 'There's Crompton Quarry about seven miles away, that'll be fine.'

'Had a look at it, have you?' Cathy's voice rises.

He shrugs. There's not a trace of bravado in what he's saying. Suddenly, Cathy's alarmed. 'If ever you did that, I'd be so cross.'

'No, you wouldn't,' says Jason, 'because I'd have the mother of all funerals. I'd hire this cathedral and everyone who's ever known me would be there. In the front row, there'd be you, Mark, Adam and Becky and Jez, though he'll have gone to the wrong church first and be an hour late.'

'And Lauren?'

'She'll slime in. She'll feel she has to be there. So she'll turn up in this black dress she'll have

149

bought from Miss Selfridge and she'll be crying, but underneath, she'll have this onion. No she won't, she'll have these spray-on tears. But as soon as the funeral's over she'll say, "Okay everyone, let's go down the pub".' He looks away again but he can't hide the pain in his face any more. It's then Cathy knows that, more than anything else in the world, she wants to help Jason. Nothing else matters to her as much as that.

'And Cathy,' he goes on, 'I'll be there at my funeral and as Lauren's leaving, I'll step out of the shadows. Only she can see me, then I'll say. . . He stops, then bursts out, 'She hasn't rung me, you know, not once in two months. No, how are you, thought I'd just check you were still breathing. It's like I don't exist any more. Nothing.'

'Maybe she's waiting for you to ring her.'

There's a flicker of hope in his eyes but then he gets up, very gently putting Tripod on to the couch. 'I don't think so. Anyway, she finished it. Not that I could give a toss, anyway. When you see her, tell her I'm going out with a professional model. Will you tell her that for me?'

'If you like,' says Cathy. She wants to cry out, I'm not just Lauren's friend. Look closer. See how much I care. But of course, the words never leave her head.

'I'll see you around, Cathy, and if I don't see you before, good luck with all your exams.'

'Thanks,' but her heart sinks at the thought of more weeks stretching ahead, without Jason in them.

Then to her surprise, he's gazing right at her. 'Your hair, you've let it grow.'

'Yes.'

'I like it. I liked it before but it looks the business now.'

She hopes she's not blushing. She's gone all fluttery. 'I had it done last week. Thanks ... oh, thanks.'

He starts to walk away.

'Look after yourself, won't you?' she says it so fervently, he looks back over his shoulder. He gives her a swift but confiding smile.

'And you, Cathy,' he says.

Adam was really surprised when Cathy asked him to order *Quadrophenia* for her. 'I wouldn't have thought that was your kind of film at all,' he said.

But Cathy just smiled mysteriously and actually, it isn't her kind of film, yet she is enjoying it. It's after midnight and her family are all asleep, so she can't play the film as loudly as it demands. But the rawness, the power, still come through. It's only when the guy starts getting disillusioned with the mods, that Cathy becomes anxious. Soon, he's going to take that ride off the cliff, isn't he? Yes, look, there he goes, faster and faster. Any second

151

now. Cathy starts breathing heavily. 'Turn back. Don't do it, not this time,' she whispers. But he doesn't listen and . . . Cathy turns away. She wishes she hadn't watched it.

She looks back and then lets out a tiny cry of joy. His bike's smashed into millions of pieces all right. But he isn't. Instead, he's walking away. She rewinds the scene, to make absolutely certain. Then, she nearly rings up Jason, she's so excited. She'll certainly tell him.

'You don't mind, do you?' asks Lauren. Cathy and Mark shake their heads. 'It's just, I hate standing about waiting, with everyone asking, did you revise that vital speech on page 47.'

'So do I,' says Cathy. 'No, we'll get right away for a few minutes. We'll go for a little walk in to town.'

It's a quarter-to-nine and Cathy has just driven Lauren, Mark and herself into college for their first A level exam, English. The entrance is already flooded with students gabbling nervously away; Lauren took one look, turned an ever paler white than she was already, and exited.

'I couldn't eat any breakfast,' says Mark. 'But I might swallow a few sweets.'

Lauren gives a shudder. 'My mum forced me to eat something. I thought I was going to throw up all over her.'

Cathy says, 'Mark, do you remember when your stomach kept rumbling in that Maths exam?'

'Cheers for reminding me about that, Cathy. It was well-embarrassing,' says Mark.

'But those exams are nothing compared with these, are they?' says Lauren. 'There's so much resting on them. Do you know, I woke up with a copy of *The Winter's Tale* in my hand. And yet, I still feel as if I'm going to walk into that hall and just forget it all.'

'No, you won't,' says Cathy, soothingly. She'd forgotten how stressed Lauren can become about things like exams. Cathy got really stressed last night, as she pictured the hall with all the exam papers laid out, everything so quiet and intense, and freezingly formal. Then the rustle of papers being turned over and that robotic voice: 'You may start.' But this morning, although she's still anxious, she feels strangely distant from it all, as if it's already happened. Lauren's definitely got the jitters, though. 'I can't help thinking how much is resting on these exams,' she says.

'I just keep wishing I'd done more revision,' says Mark. 'But I've been so busy with other things. I mean, every day at college, there've been people to see, meetings to go to ... Anyway, it's too late now.'

'Look you two, stop depressing yourselves and breathe in some of this fresh air,' says Cathy.

'Cartford hasn't got any fresh air,' says Lauren. All around them shops are starting to show signs of life. They watch a girl setting up the flowers outside her shop. 'That'll be me,' says Lauren gloomily, 'when I fail all my exams.'

'Some people enjoy working in shops,' says Cathy. And it's then she spots Jason putting some new trainers in his shop window. Lauren sees him too, for she says, 'Just walk past. Pretend you haven't seen him, not now, please.'

But Cathy has no intention of ignoring Jason. Last Saturday she and Lauren had gone for a drink to give themselves a respite from revising. And who should be in The White Hart but Jason, with Mark and Tara and some other people Cathy dimly recognised from the sports shop. It turned out that Jason was celebrating; he'd just been officially made assistant manager. Cathy went over to congratulate Jason and stayed for about half-an-hour, leaving Lauren on her own. She felt bad about that but she couldn't ignore Jason, then or now, so she accompanies Mark over to the sports shop. To her surprise, Lauren follows, at a distance.

'Big day, then,' says Jason, grinning.

'You needn't look so happy about it,' says Cathy.

'No, you'll be all right, you'll walk it,' says Jason.

'I wish,' says Mark.

'Anyway, I can always get you a job at my sports shop,' Jason says airily. Cathy waits for Lauren

154

to make a sarcastic comment but she doesn't say anything. They stand chatting for a couple of minutes. Jason seems most relaxed, lounging against the shop window in his track suit, although, Cathy notices, he keeps darting glances at Lauren.

Then, Mark says, 'It's five-to-nine, we'd better go.'

'Good luck, then,' says Jason. Then, he whispers, 'Good luck, Lauren.'

'Thanks,' she says and gives him a small smile. 'Goodbye,' she adds, as they trail back to college.

But Jason doesn't move. He wants to let the full glory of that moment sink in. She spoke to him. First time, in ten weeks. And, as a kind of bonus, she smiled too. This is what he'd been waiting for, so impatiently, so desperately.

At first, he'd been convinced she'd ring to apologise. 'I was a bit hasty, wasn't I? I never meant to finish with you. It's just . . .' Then Jason would smile understandingly. But there were no calls, no letters, nothing. She wasn't missing him at all.

That's when he thought, to hell with her. He did so much for her and gave her 100% loyalty, never so much as looking at another girl. And she just threw it away. TO HELL WITH HER! Then he went out with other girls, as beautiful as Lauren. Classy girls, too. And he really wanted to get involved with them. Yet, the truth was, he couldn't feel anything for any of them. Shocking, actually. But there it is.

And sometimes he'd see Lauren walking through the town. Be honest, he spent all day watching out for her. And then, he'd torment himself by asking, just what is she thinking, what's going on in her head? Is she missing him? Once, he deliberately bumped in to her and she couldn't even look at him properly. Was this because she was feeling insanely guilty over what she'd done? Or was she only embarrassed at meeting an ex-boyfriend, a ghost from her past?

If just once she'd linger outside the sports shop. If only she'd just ask him, 'How are you doing, then?' Something, anything, to stop him from going insane. And now, she has given him a sign. She's spoken to him – and smiled. She wants him back. But she's too proud to say so.

She won't accept the blame for what's happened, will she? But then, that's Lauren for you. She won't accept the blame for anything. But it doesn't matter. She still needs him. That's what's important. And Jason the Bold will make it all right and save her again, this time from her pride. For he's going to ring her. Make the first gesture. And as soon as the idea hits him it knocks everything out of his head. All he can think about is dialling that number. He just can't wait. For ten weeks they've been stalled; now, at last, they're moving again.

Jason doesn't have a lunch hour and leaves work early instead. At five o'clock, he's in his house, pacing by the phone. He wants to ring her before her dad gets home. He'd hate to have to talk to her dad. So five o'clock's the ideal time to ring. He'll ask her about the exam and then, well, he'll improvise. Do it then. Ring her. Save her, just like you've done before. All day, he's wanted to ring her. But now, he's lost his bottle. Go on, do it, now. Her dad will be home soon.

He stands right in front of the phone. What are you afraid of? Feelings can't just die, can they? She needed you before. She needs you now. She's probably desperate for you to ring her.

Jason snatches up the phone and dials the number furiously. He'll probably get her mum, but that's cool, he can handle it. But in fact, it's Lauren who answers. This throws him for a moment.

'Hello, Lauren, it's me.'

'Oh, hello, Jason,' Her voice sounds surprisingly warm. It's going to be all right.

'Just rang up to ask how the exam went?'

'Okay, I think I messed up the first question but otherwise it was all right. Cathy ran out of time. Mark didn't like the questions on *The Winter's Tale* but I was expecting something on Leontes's jealousy.' She sounds amazingly chatty, considering they haven't spoken for over ten whole weeks.

Jason gathers confidence. 'I've got some good news for you. I've just decided who I'd like to have a drink with on Saturday night – and your name was at the top of the list . . . if you're free.'

There's a brief pause, then Lauren says, 'Actually, I'm not. I'm going out to see a play.'

Jason longs to ask who with, but restrains himself. 'What about another night then?' His voice is tighter now.

'All the other nights I'm revising. I'm only allowed out one night a week at the moment.'

Jason should stop, while he's still got some dignity left, only he can't. 'How about just meeting up for a coffee?' Jason attempts a laugh. 'Or can't you bear even half-an-hour of my company now?'

Lauren laughs too. A horrible, embarrassed laugh. What is he doing? Why can't he just ring off? He'll be begging her in a minute.

'I just thought it would be good if we met up for a chat and a laugh. Nothing heavy.' He stops. Lauren should be speaking.

Finally she does. 'I'd rather not.'

It's like a fist landing right on his throat. He can barely croak, 'All right then.'

'I am sorry,' she says.

He can't speak at all now. But it doesn't matter for she's already rung off.

*

Cathy, Lauren and Mark edge forward warily. It's just gone nine o'clock and another riotously hot August day is checking in. But they couldn't tell you if a full-scale blizzard was raging. Their eyes are fixed on the doors of the college.

'Shall we be brave?' asks Mark. He's itching to go inside and yet, he's dead scared. He wants to know, get it over with, and yet . . . Suddenly, all three of them leg it inside.

At the reception desk, the woman who's always there is saying, in her best speaking-clock tones, 'Yes, the A level results will be posted to you today but if you want to come in, we are open from . . .' while they spin around in search of . . . 'Here they are,' cries Mark, pointing.

And there, plastered across the walls, which normally contain timetables and details of room changes which no one ever reads, are hundreds of horribly official white sheets, each bearing a name at the top. They scramble forward. The exam results stretch right down the wall.

'My name. I can't find my name,' cries Lauren.

'You're up here,' says Cathy. 'It's alphabetical. Oh Lauren, you got . . .'

'No, don't tell me,' screeches Lauren. She sways forward, quite dizzy with nerves. She can't look. Yes, she can. She squints at her name, then lets out a scream. 'No,' she cries, 'I don't believe it.' Check it, check you haven't read someone else's

159

result by mistake. Wouldn't that be awful. But yes, it's true, she's got an A in English and an A in Communications, 2 As – and a C in Geography. She lets out another scream.

'Sssh,' calls the woman at reception, while ten phones jangle furiously around her.

'Sorry,' says Lauren.

The woman smiles. 'Well, at least someone's pleased,' she says.

Lauren turns to Cathy. 'What did you get?'

'A grade B in English, a C in Communications and a B in Geography.' Cathy's beaming. 'Much better than I thought, and you did brilliantly, didn't you?'

'Yes,' cries Lauren. 'You saw it too, didn't you? I wasn't hallucinating or anything?'

Cathy laughs, they hug each other excitedly, then turn to Mark. He's not smiling. 'Anyone want to swap?' he says. 'I got a C in English, D in Communications and an E in History, so it's goodbye Brighton.'

'Why, what did you need, 2 Cs?' asks Cathy. He nods gloomily.

'But you're only one grade out,' says Cathy. 'Maybe they'll still . . .'

'I doubt it,' says Mark. 'Still, I can always go through clearing. Anyway, I'm not really surprised. It'd have been a miracle if I'd done better, because I never really worked. I had so much else to do.'

160

'At least you passed,' says Lauren. 'Look at some of these results. This girl here, got none.'

'That's terrible,' says Mark smiling.

'And someone else here has got 3 Us, and what did Tricia Williams get? Ha! I beat her. She only got a D, despite all her private coaching from Grant. He'll be wild when he sees I got an A, won't he?'

Cathy and Mark nod, grinning. They look up what everyone else in their group got. Then a girl rushes up to the notice-board, stares at her name, gives a little cry, then rushes away again. 'Oh dear,' says Cathy, 'she doesn't look so happy.'

'Exams are awful really, aren't they?' says Mark. 'They give you so much grief. I know her vaguely. When I was standing for president, she came up and told me she was definitely for me.'

'She's insane then,' says Lauren. 'No, joke. Listen, we're all going back to my place for breakfast, aren't we?'

'Yeah, come on,' says Cathy. She links arms with Mark. 'You're not too disappointed, are you?'

'I'm not disappointed at all. I knew I'd fouled-up that last History paper and – no, I'm not disappointed. It's my parents I feel sorry for. You see, I did really well with my GCSEs and they think I'm a bit of a genius. I'm only glad they're on holiday. I've got to ring them as soon as I know,' he winces, 'but at least it won't be as bad as telling them face to face.'

Lauren calls out to the woman at reception, 'Goodbye, you'll probably never see us again. Bet you're sorry about that.'

'But you will see me again,' cries Mark. 'I've got to come in to advise the new executive.' The woman waves a hand, then goes back to the phones, and chants, 'Yes, the A level results will be posted today but if you want to come in, the college is open from . . .'

Cathy drives them to Lauren's house. Lauren races up the drive where her mum is waiting. Then, Lauren's mum sweeps Lauren up into her arms, while declaring, 'Well done darling! Oh, well done!' Lauren's mum hugs Cathy too and smiles sympathetically at Mark. Then she says, 'I'll go and get the breakfast started. But first, Lauren . . . he's just waiting by that phone.' No more needs to be said. And soon Lauren is talking away to her dad, her eyes shining excitedly, while Lauren's mum tells Cathy, 'He's been so anxious. He hardly slept at all last night. For he knew how much these results meant to Lauren.' Then Cathy has a word with Lauren's dad, his congratulations booming around the room.

After this, Lauren's mum brings in a special celebratory breakfast: no bacon, of course, but fried

162

eggs on toast, tomatoes, mushrooms – and a bottle of champagne.

Lauren pours herself another glass and announces, 'I've only had one glass and already I feel . . .'

'Drunk,' prompts Mark.

'No, but strange. Very strange. And I just can't believe my exam results. I'm still expecting someone to ring up and say, "Sorry Lauren, there's a misprint and really you got 2 Ds".'

'You'd never have got 2 Ds,' says Cathy.

'If I hadn't broken up with Jason, I wouldn't even have got 2 Ds. I'd probably be doing re-sits next year.'

'No, you wouldn't,' says Cathy promptly.

Lauren leans forward. 'Yes, I would, Cathy. After Jason and I split up I did so much work and it was that work which made the difference.' Her voice rises, 'It was, you know.' Then Lauren gives her a look as if to say, Agree with me, please.

Cathy persists. 'You'd have got As whether you'd broken up with Jason or not. You're just naturally talented.' It sounds as if Cathy's paying her a compliment. In a way she is. But she's also saying, Lauren was needlessly cruel to Jason. And that just isn't true.

'Cathy, you don't know how little work I did when I was with Jason. He hated me doing home-work.'

163

'Like you say, I don't know,' says Cathy and changes the subject.

Then Mark goes and rings his parents. He dials the number, hears his mother's voice, and slams the phone down. 'I can't tell her,' he says. 'She'll be so gutted.' After ten minutes of gentle persuasion from Cathy, Lauren and Lauren's mum, Mark does ring back.

'Hello, Mum, I did rubbish,' he says. But when he puts the phone down he's smiling. 'She was all right about it. She says, I've got to ring up the college, get some advice.'

So Mark rings up the college and gets an interview with the Careers Advisor for half-past eleven. Lauren's mum drives him to college and Lauren goes too, while Cathy sets off home. The first person she sees there is Giles.

Yesterday, he sneezed four times, so clearly he is in need of urgent medical attention. There he lolls in the lounge, radio blaring, table stacked high with papers. Wherever he goes, he leaves a mess. Her mum dashes out of the kitchen. She looks at Cathy expectantly.

'Two Bs and a C – Bs in English and Geography and C in Communications.'

'Wonderful, oh, you clever girl!' Her mum rushes forward, hesitates, then kisses her lightly on the cheek. 'That's marvellous news . . . Giles, did you hear that?' She propels Cathy into the lounge doorway. 'Cathy's passed all her A levels, 2 Bs and a C.'

Giles switches on a smile. 'That's certainly good news. It's always gratifying when hard works pays off.' He shakes her by the hand and says, 'Those grades are good enough to get you into university, aren't they?'

'Of course they are,' says Cathy's mum.

He considers some more. 'It's a shame you didn't apply this year, isn't it? But you can probably still get in.'

'I don't want to get in,' hisses Cathy. 'I want a year out first.'

'To do what, exactly?' asks Giles.

'I don't know yet,' says Cathy. 'Why, are you trying to get rid of me?'

Giles shakes his head sadly. 'I just thought it would be a shame to waste a year.'

'I know what you thought,' mutters Cathy, marching into the kitchen. Cathy's mum follows her. 'Oh, Cathy, you don't give Giles a chance. You're so touchy with him. He's on your side. He's trying to help.'

'All right, Mum, I'm sorry,' says Cathy wearily, wishing she'd gone back to college with Lauren and Mark.

'You and Giles have been getting on so well lately, haven't you . . . and that's meant a lot to me, you know.' Cathy looks away. She and Giles have been pretending to get on well, which isn't the same thing at all. Deep down, she suspects Giles doesn't like her any more than she likes him. But most of the time she and Giles wear masks. They put them on now, as she and her mum have a celebratory cup of tea with the rosy-cheeked flu victim.

She leaves her mum fussing around him, while she wonders who she can share her good news with. Jason? She's popped into the shop to see him quite a few times. They always have a good chat and, a couple of times, they seemed on the edge of something else. She felt he was about to confide in her. But anyway, he didn't and now he's gone on holiday, apparently. No one knows exactly where. He keeps disappearing these days.

So she rings Jez. She hasn't seen that much of him lately, either, for he's back on the building site to 'earn some more dosh'. But he did say he'd be home today and told her to ring him.

He sounds really chuffed by her news. 'I knew you'd do it,' he says. 'I had total confidence in you.' Then he asks, 'Are you available this afternoon?'

She laughs. 'That depends what for?'

'Afternoon tea.'

'How civilised.'

'Oh yeah, I'm very civilised. Besides, I want to ask you something.'

'What?'

166

'Tell you this afternoon.'

'Jez, tell me now.'

He gives his strange, wheezing chuckle. 'No, it's too important to say over the phone.'

Cathy's bursting with curiosity now. 'I hate it when people do that.'

'I know.'

'Tell me.'

He wheezes down the phone again. 'See you around half-two, then. Got to go. Congratulations again – and don't die of curiosity, will you?'

At half-past two exactly, Cathy is outside Jez's house. It is his mum who answers the door. She beams at Cathy. 'Well done, my dear. Jeremy told me your good news.' Cathy stifles a laugh. If there's one name which doesn't suit Jez, it's his real one. 'Jeremy's in the lounge, waiting for you,' continues his mum and she gives Cathy what can only be described as a gleeful smile. Cathy's never seen Jez's mum look so happy.

Cathy walks into the lounge, then does a double-take. 'Jez, your beard.'

'What about it?'

'It's gone.'

'Has it?' he touches his chin. 'So it has, fancy that. Never know what's going to drop off next, do you? I just woke up this morning and it had gone. Been looking for it all day. So if you see a spare

167

beard ... A very serious question now. Do you want me to stick it back on?'

'Oh no. Now I can see that you've got quite young skin really. And you look much more open and ...'

'Sexy,' prompts Jez.

Cathy had been going to say, 'vulnerable' but she accepts 'sexy' – sexier, anyway.

'Mmm, yes, I'd say so.' Then she takes in his white shirt and clean denim trousers. 'You look positively smart.' He bows and grins. She grins too, then asks, 'But what's all this for?'

It's then his mum reappears with a trolley piled high with food. 'I'll leave it here, then you can help yourselves, can't you.'

'Cheers, Mum.'

'It all looks delicious,' says Cathy. After Jez's mum disappears, Cathy asks, 'Is anyone else coming round?'

'No.'

'But we'll never eat all this.'

'You're not leaving this room until you do. So start stuffing your face, young lady.'

He gives Cathy a plate. 'Well, I'll try some choc-olate cake, although I shouldn't,' she says. Then Jez pours out the tea, his hand shaking slightly as he does so. Cathy watches him curiously. He hands her a cup of weak tea. 'Come on, tell me,' she says. 'What's the mystery?'

'You're very impatient.'

'Jez, do you want this cup of tea over your head?'

'All right. I'm leaving for Italy next week.'

'Oh Jez, how could you, running out on me again.'

'No, I'm not, I half-asked you before. This time, I'm doing it properly. Cathy, I want you to come with me.'

She stares at him incredulously.

'I thought we could have a nose around Italy, then I'd show you Germany. I've saved enough for our plane fare.'

'I'll pay for myself,' says Cathy promptly. Then she says, 'But I can't just go.'

'Why not?'

'Why? Well, there's . . . there's Adam and Becky's wedding, for a start. We've got to be here for that.'

'I'd forgotten about that.'

'Jez, we only got the invites last week.'

'Okay, when's the wedding?'

'September 20th.'

'Right, I'll wait for you. But the second Adam and Becky's wedding finishes, we go. Come on, it'll be a crack.' Jez rubs his hands together. 'And no more excuses . . . or my mum will never forgive you.'

'She knows, doesn't she?'

'Yeah, well she got a bit suspicious when she

saw me washing one of my shirts. She thinks you're a lovely girl. If you turn me down again, I don't think my mum will ever get over it.' Then he snatches up her cup, goes over to the trolley and starts slopping tea into it. He turns round to see Cathy standing beside him. 'Jez, you make a lousy cup of tea,' she says, 'but despite that, I'd love to go with you.'

'You would? Magic.' He's standing grinning at her, rubbing his hands furiously.

She leans forward and kisses him lightly on the lips. It feels so much better without the beard,' she says.

He takes her hand. 'Cathy – this is the happiest day of my mum's life – and mine.'

Lauren doesn't think she can stand it.

Her parents are upstairs getting ready; they're taking Lauren out for a meal to celebrate her good news. And they are just bubbling with happiness; her dad keeps calling out silly jokes to Lauren and her mum, hissing with laughter before he reaches the punch-line.

Lauren flees downstairs. She doesn't want her parents to suss out what she's really feeling. They wouldn't understand. Not that she does, either. It's all so annoying – and confusing.

The phones goes. Lauren hopes it's not for her. She doesn't want to have to talk to anyone and put on her, 'Yes, I'm so thrilled' voice.' Then she hears her mum say, 'Hello, Cathy dear, you sound excited. Yes, I'll just call her for you.' But Lauren can't talk to Cathy, of all people.

So instead, she bolts out of the door and runs as fast as she can. What was Cathy ringing her about? She doesn't know and doesn't care.

For it was Cathy who . . . Why couldn't she just have agreed with Lauren today? Especially as it was perfectly obvious that Lauren wouldn't have passed her A levels if she'd still been going out with Jason. Yet Cathy, her so-called best friend, has to poison everything.

Lauren's now pounding through Dell Wood. It's just gone six o'clock but it is still scorching hot. The air feels heavy, uncomfortable, stale. Just ahead of her looms their hut. Now she's acting like a demented homing pigeon. Why has she come back here?

Years ago, Lauren used to hide away in the hut when she was unhappy and confused. But today marks Lauren's glorious triumph. Her A level results are everything she'd hoped for. For a few minutes she was elated, then she felt horribly flat. Now, she's on the edge of tears.

She turns the combination lock and steps inside. The last time she'd been here was for Adam and Becky's engagement party. There's the empty wine bottle and there are those plates they never got

171

around to washing. She wonders if anyone's been back here since the engagement party. She doubts it.

She gazes around, her eyes finally settling on a piece of antique lettering, THIS IS PRIVATE PROPERTY AND BELONGS TO JEZ, LAUREN, ADAM, MARK, CATHY AND JASON (BLAZE).

Private property! How absurd that sounds now. And yet, this hut did belong to them. Perhaps it always will. She'd certainly hate to think of anyone else tramping about in here, peering at their message, wondering who they all were. No, this is our own private kingdom, with Jason as its ruler. Right from the start he took charge. They were always running to him. 'Jason, what do I do . . . ? Jason will you . . . Jason.'

Now she knows why she is here. He's everywhere in this hut, every corner is crammed with memories. There he is at one of their meetings, declaring, 'On our own we're okay, but together, we're something.' Now she remembers him coming up to her at a party, saying, 'I heard you were pretty,' giving this goofy smile, then adding, 'and all the rumours were true.' First words he ever spoke to her. How old were they then? Eleven?

She had to wait nearly four years before he asked her out. It was the day after he scored about a thousand goals in some football match and he steamed up to her, saying, 'Yesterday you saw me having a bit of a heyday, so now at last, I can dare to ask you out.' That night she thought she would die of happiness.

She sways back. But there's no stopping the flood of memories now. There he is, carrying her out of Swanks, that was the night he rescued her from Grant and she lost her shoes – never found them. Then she sees him pulling a picture off the wall in a café because she likes it. He was mad but he'd have done anything for her. If she'd told him to jump in the river, he'd have done it.

And now, there they are together, in the hut. It was the night he rescued her from Grant. He told her it was he who'd sent her all the flowers. Then he said, 'I owe you a massive apology for what I did to you at your fifteenth birthday.'

Her fifteenth birthday. Will she ever forget that night? That was when Jason turned up with another girl on his arm. She just tore out of her party and ran. She came and sat in here, didn't she, and then . . .

She rushes outside. Then she starts digging away at all the stones and rocks by the hut. They scratch against her hands and some mud falls on to her dress but for once she doesn't care, doesn't even notice. Where is it? She's certain she buried it around here. Yes, here it is.

She pulls it up, rips off the plastic casing,

fumbles with the red ribbon, then finally unfurls the scroll. 'WE THE UNDERSIGNED, SWEAR TO STAY TOGETHER, DEFEND EACH OTHER AND DEFEAT EACH OTHERS' ENEMIES,' and there were their signatures, each joined to the next, to show how they could never be separated, and underneath, all their names in capitals.

But one name is missing. There are only tiny holes where Jason's name was. Lauren stares down at the document, her eyes glistening with tears, as she again watches herself stabbing away at every letter of Jason's name with her make-up pencil. How far away that moment seems now. It's as if she's watching someone she hardly knows at all.

Then she'd loved Jason so much. Then he was everything to her. Nothing else even mattered. And now, she's let him go. Her hands cover her face as she rocks back and forth. Poor Jason. She was so cold to him when he rang up. But he rang at the wrong time. It was the first day of the exams. She had weeks of revising ahead of her, but he never understood that. She *had* to pass those A levels. And now she's passed them and all she wants to do is go back, back to when Jason filled all her dreams.

Jason – but she can't bear even to think about him now. It hurts too much. So she just slumps forward while the tears stream down her face. What is she to do? Go back, beg his forgiveness. He'll still take her back. Yes, that's what she'll do.

Only, the break-up wasn't all her fault, was it? Jason wanted too much from her. He never left anything for her, did he?

And if she'd stayed with Jason, what would she have done, what would she have seen? Nothing. She'd have been grounded in Cartford all her life. But she wants more, deserves more. She sits up, wiping her eyes with her sleeve. When you break up with someone, they say, watch out for the relapses, don't they? That's all she's had, a relapse.

She leans over, picks up the scroll and then feels another stab of pain, and it's so sharp it makes her cry out: Jason, my darling, I did love you so much but . . . dreams change, you see. They have to. Otherwise, you'd never move on, never grow. And Jason, you do cling on to people, don't you? You clung on so hard that I couldn't breathe. You smothered me. And despite everything you say, you'd do it again. In the end, we'd just make each other miserable. That's why it could never work with us, not for long, anyway. That's why we've got to let each other go. Not that you'll ever really leave me. I'll carry you around in my heart . . . one day I'll write and tell you that. Not yet. But one day I will. I promise.

She'd better get back. Her parents will be wondering where she's gone. She's starting to feel hungry too. She rolls up the scroll. Will anyone ever dig it up again? Maybe they've all forgotten about it. No, Jason will remember and one day . . . that's why she should . . . yes, it's the least she can do.

She gets up, goes back into the hut, brings out one of the marker pens Adam kept there and underneath her name, prints, AND JASON. 'See Jason,' she whispers, 'I've given you back.'

9

"Friends Forever"

Becky jumps awake. What's the time now? Half-past five. Twenty minutes later than the last time. There are just so many thoughts racing through her head and her room seems too small to contain them all. She has to get up for a while. So she creeps downstairs and sits at the big table in the dining room.

On this table are arrayed the wedding presents: decanters, vases, cutlery, table lamps, saucepans, linen, food mixers and . . . she picks up one of the wine glasses. In six hours time this wine glass will be officially theirs. In six hours time, she will be a newly-wed.

She sits staring into space trying to hold that fact in her head. But it keeps slipping away. Finally, she trails back upstairs and dozes off for another twenty minutes.

Now it's nearly seven o'clock. Thursday 20th September can officially begin. She's excited and yet she wishes it were all over. She wonders if Adam is awake yet. From tonight, she'll always know when Adam is awake.

There's a tap on her door and then her mum says, 'How did I know you'd be awake,' and gives her sing-song laugh.

Becky smiles, 'How long have you been awake?'

'I heard you going downstairs.'

'Oh, I'm sorry.'

'No, I nearly joined you, but then I thought you might like to be on your own.' She draws the curtains.

'What sort of day is it?' asks Becky.

'One or two unhealthy-looking grey clouds but all the weather forecasts say it'll be sunny this morning. Rain isn't predicted until late this afternoon, by which time you'll be well on your way to Paris.'

'Yes, I will, won't I,' says Becky. What a day this is going to be; first stop eleven-thirty, Cartford Registry Office, then one o'clock the wedding reception at a sixteenth-century hotel, The Old Lodge, and at four o'clock she and Adam are flying to Paris for a long weekend, a wedding present from her mum.

'By the way,' says her mum, just a little too

178

casually, 'the post has been. There's a card from your father.'

'About time.'

'It was posted first class, on Tuesday, actually,' says her mum. 'There's also a cheque.'

'How much?'

'A hundred pounds.'

'We'll take it, because we need it,' says Becky. 'I'm just so glad he's not coming . . . he'd be there judging everyone, setting himself up as this great man. Mum, tell me, how could someone as wonderful as you marry someone so utterly gross?'

'He had his moments,' says her mum, lightly.

'But, on your wedding day, did you have any doubts?'

Her mum laughs. 'As I remember, I spent the morning before I got married – a beautiful spring morning it was – going round my garden, in a kind of trance, gazing at every flower, every leaf. I just felt so in tune with the universe. I saw everything smeared with romance. I was a real vaseline-lens girl, then. But I'm not sorry.' She sits down on Becky's bed. 'Besides, I think we are drawn to people we are going to learn things from. No, I'm not sorry,' she repeats. 'Your nan had deep, deep doubts about the marriage. I'd watch her swallowing down her feelings. But she didn't want to be one of those mothers. By the way, I don't either.'

'But Mum, you haven't got any doubts about

Adam and me now, have you?' Becky's voice rises. 'I know you *were* unhappy about us, weren't you?'

'I wasn't unhappy, exactly. I just felt you had so much life to live, so much potential and I didn't want to see you narrowing your life down.'

'And now?' asks Becky.

'What's that saying? The sweetness of life is terribly perishable. It's true. That's why marriage is always the greatest gamble in the world. I do like Adam very much. But to be honest, what I think is unimportant now. And once you're married, I'm going to stand back so far from you and Adam, you'll think I don't care any more. I still do, of course. But I know you've got to work it out for yourselves. That's the only way you'll grow together. But before I abdicate, I'm going to issue one last edict and insist you eat some breakfast, all right? We've got lots of time.' Becky finds that phrase oddly comforting.

She and her mum have a lovely, leisurely breakfast of tea and toast and everything feels more like a Sunday than her wedding day. Then she has a bath, her mum drives her down to the hairdresser where Cathy and Lauren pop in to say hello, then her mum brings her back home again. After this, her mum goes to the station to meet Nan. Becky opens her wardrobe and stares at her cream suit with the blue and cream polka dot buttons. She'd bought it in this boutique, just outside Cartford,

180

with Lauren and Cathy and her mum. And she'd been so excited. But now, it looms menacingly.

She closes the wardrobe door again. Now she hasn't got lots of time. In half-an-hour the car will be here and then there can be no looking back, ever again.

Already, it's as if a wall is going up between her and everyone else. Even her mum. And she's not ready. It's all going too fast. Once she'd enjoyed the speed. But now, it scares her. She can't go through with this, can she?

Just why is she getting married anyway? What will she get out of it? She's not moving into a new house, just another room in her mum's house. She'll still be doing the same boring job at the *Pizza Paradiso*, with the highlight, going to evening class. Wow!

What else has she got to look forward to? More hassles, that's for certain. Right from the start it's been nothing but hassles, has it? Secret meetings, Mark having to pretend to be her boyfriend, Adam's parents trying to break them up – even now they don't know if his mum will turn up at the wedding. Then, months and months of saving for Thomas. Thomas! She gives a little cry. Then she hears her mum come back with her nan. Nan calls up to her, then her mum asks, 'How are you getting on? Do you need a hand?'

'No, I'm fine,' says Becky. 'I'll be down in a

minute.' In a kind of trance, she puts on the cream suit. It cost enough, so she may as well wear it, even though she can't go through with it. She glances at herself in the mirror. How does she look? Hard to tell for she can't stop shaking.

To try and steady herself she thrusts her hands down her pockets. There's an envelope in the right pocket. She pulls it out and then sees it has BECKY scrawled across it and underneath, NOT TO BE OPENED UNTIL YOUR WEDDING DAY.

She tears open the envelope. Inside is a sheet of paper on which is written: DEDICATED TO BECKY:

I'll haul you to dry land and love you more,
Jump in,
If you trust me,
Jump in,
And we'll float away,
Kiss everything else away,
And I'll never let you go,
Away.
Adam.

She reads the words over and over and even when she finally slips the poem back into her pocket, the words are dancing around her head. Funny, at the time she thought it was strange the way Adam was so keen to see what she was wearing. 'I have to inspect it,' he said. That's when he must have slipped the envelope into her pocket, as if he knew, this morning, she'd need him with her.

She puts on her cream, leather gloves. Adam, I got scared. I am scared. But you are the right one for me. I know it now. I always knew it, really. And I'll never let you go, either.

She gets up and looks out of her window. What a smiling, shining world it is. Then she hears her mum calling her again. 'I'm ready,' she cries.

Adam is lying back in his bath, trying to relax, when the door bursts open and Mark appears, brandishing a video camera.

'Come on, smile Adam,' cries Mark.

'Get out of here,' yells Adam. He picks up a bar of soap, lunges forward, and fires it at the camera.

'Now that's excellent,' says Mark. 'A very revealing shot of you there and a brilliant opening to the wedding video. Thanks a lot. Bye.'

'Mark,' calls Adam after him, 'do you want to live?'

Mark just laughs his way down the stairs. 'I'm going to send this film to The Chippendales. I'm sure they'll snap you up.' He laughs again. 'I'm now going to pick up our carnations.'

An hour later he is carefully pinning a red carnation on to Adam's double-breasted suit. Then he looks at Adam's paisley tie and shakes his head. 'I know, I can never do ties up properly,' says Adam. 'I hate ties.'

'Better let the maestro do it,' says Mark. 'See, you want a much better knot than that.'

'This reminds me of my first date with Becky,' says Adam. 'You practically dressed me that night. And you booked the table. You even gave me polos to keep my breath fresh for afterwards . . . and I just reeked of aftershave. I couldn't have got through that evening without you, you know.'

Mark looks embarrassed but chuffed. Then he asks, 'Not too tight, is it?'

'No, I just can't see the point of ties. At school, it was like the worst sin in the world not to wear a tie. How long have we got, Mark?'

'Plenty of time yet,' says Mark.

Adam stares out of his window. 'It was good news about Sheffield, wasn't it?

'Yeah, at first I thought I wasn't going to get in anywhere. But Sheffield, being a place of real discernment, said, "Mark, baby, you want to do English here, well come right in".'

'You're looking pretty happy these days,' says Adam.

'I suppose I am. I feel like my life's falling into place. And now I'm going to Sheffield, where no one knows me, which will be great. And I'm going to be quite different to my normal personality. I'm not going to jump out at people any more. I'll be much more reserved and calm . . . a bit like you, actually. I'll be quiet but cool. And I'll have all these girls just going mad with lust for the rippling hunk, that is, yours truly.'

The doorbell rings and three familiar voices are heard chatting to Mark's mum, then tearing upstairs. Lauren appears in Mark's bedroom first. 'Oh, don't they both look yummy in their suits.'

'Men always look better dressed up,' says Cathy.

'I suppose that's a dig at me,' says Jez, who's wearing a grey jacket, white shirt and black trousers. 'No offence, Adam, but there's no point in buying a suit just for this.'

'I did,' says Lauren, who's wearing a stunning pink suit.

'Come on, then, give us a twirl, Lauren,' says Mark. 'And you Cathy.' Cathy's wearing a powder-blue silk two-piece.

'You both look all right, don't you?' says Mark.

'And we saw Becky in the hairdresser's,' says Lauren, flopping down on Mark's bed.

'How is she?' asks Adam, at once.

'Just fine,' says Cathy, 'and her hair looks lovely.'

'You've always liked skinhead haircuts, haven't you?' says Jez.

'Ignore him,' says Cathy. 'I can't believe I'm going away with him this afternoon.' Then she asks Mark, 'You haven't seen Jason, have you?'

'No, I went into the sports shop yesterday and they said he was ill.'

'That's what they told me,' says Cathy. 'But I went around to his house and his mum didn't know where he was. She said she never knows where he is these days . . . He will turn up today, won't he?'

'He wouldn't miss this,' says Jez.

'No, he'll be here,' says Mark. 'Jason never lets you down.'

Lauren changes the subject. 'Do you realise, Mark, this is the first time I've ever been in your bedroom. It's quite big, isn't it? I am surprised,' she giggles. 'I don't know, I just feel so nervous and I'm not even getting married. How do you feel, Adam?'

He grins. 'I'm sweating something evil.'

'Aaah, poor Adam,' coos Lauren.

'You can still back out, mate, it's not too late,' says Jez. Then as Cathy and Lauren glare at him, he says, 'Joke.'

Mark's mother walks in. 'Don't you all look smart.' She turns to Cathy and Jez. 'And you're both off to Italy this afternoon, I hear?'

'Yes, that's right,' says Cathy.

'How long for?' asks Mrs Appleton.

'Until Christmas,' say Cathy.

'Maybe longer,' adds Jez.

'I'm going away tomorrow,' says Lauren. 'I'm

renting this house in Birmingham with three other girls, so I'm taking some of my stuff up.'

'That should be wicked,' says Jez, 'you having to share with three other girls.'

'What do you mean?' says Lauren. 'Are you being horrible to me?'

'Yes,' says Jez, laughing. 'No, I'm being unfair. I'm sure you'll be very easy to get along with,' and he laughs again. Soon everyone is joining in.

Lauren, half-laughing, half-indignant, says, 'After this wedding, I'm not talking to any of you again.'

'Is that a promise?' says Jez.

'Actually, I suppose we'd better think about moving,' says Mark's mum. Immediately all the laughing stops until Mark says, 'Okay, Mum, we'll just wait for you to get changed.'

'But I am . . .' begins his mum. She sees Mark grinning away at her. 'What would you do with a son like mine?'

'She loves me really,' says Mark.

Now everyone is hovering by the door. Adam says, 'It's okay me leaving all my stuff here, isn't it, Mrs. Appleton?' As he says it, Adam can't help feeling a pang, again. Picking up all his things and moving out of his home yesterday was much worse than he'd expected. There were no embarrassing scenes. In fact, his parents didn't really say anything. Yet, as he piled his suitcases into Cathy's car, it seemed as if he were running out on his family. That's why he left his motorbike behind. He had to leave something. What a total let-down he's been to his parents. He can't blame them for not coming to the wedding.

And then, when he was depositing his suitcases round at Becky's, and his wedding case at Mark's, he felt like a refugee, having to live in other people's homes, dependent on their charity. Everyone's been very nice. Mark's mum is telling him now to leave the cases here for as long as he wants. He is grateful. He just hates having to be grateful.

As they pile outside, Lauren is saying, 'You can't park at the registry office, you know. We'll probably have to walk miles.' Lauren's prediction is proved correct. They have to walk from the multi-storey car-park in Cartford town centre to one of its dingier side-streets, where the registry office, a grey little building, blends in perfectly.

'That's tacky,' says Adam, pointing at the 'open' sign in the window by the registry office door.

'It looks just like my dentist's,' says Jez.

'I feel really over-dressed standing here like this,' says Lauren. Stray passers-by carrying shopping gawp at them curiously. 'Yes, go on, have a good look,' murmurs Lauren.

But then, right on time, a white Rolls Royce sweeps majestically into view and out steps Becky's mum, Becky's nan, looking elegant and astonishingly youthful, and finally, Becky herself, in her cream suit and holding a huge bouquet of red roses.

'Hubba, hubba,' murmurs Mark to Adam.

'What?'

'You remember that film, where every time Steve Martin saw a really gorgeous woman . . .'

'Oh yeah,' interrupts Adam. 'I remember.' He gazes at Becky again. 'That's hubba, hubba, times a thousand.' She looks such a vision, he feels suddenly shy. He lets Lauren, Cathy, Jez and Mark greet and kiss Becky first while he talks to Becky's mum and is introduced to Becky's nan. But then, finally, there she is. 'Hello, Adam,' she says softly. And he feels as if he hasn't seen her for days, weeks.

'I found your poem,' she says. 'I read it over and over.' Then, before she can say anything else, Mark is zooming his video camera in their direction and Becky's mum is suggesting they all wait inside.

They crowd inside the foyer which boasts pale yellow walls and a dead plant in the corner. Meanwhile, more guests arrive, a blobby-faced uncle and aunt of Becky's, Lauren's parents (her father vigorously shaking hands with everyone present), and then two more people arrive and hover awkwardly in the doorway. Adam immediately rushes over to them.

'Look, there's Adam's mum and brother,' says Jez to Cathy.

'I'm so glad they turned up,' says Cathy.

Jez studies her. 'Are you all right? You look a bit pale.'

'No, I'm fine, thanks. I'm just a bit worried about Jason.'

'He'll be here,' says Jez. Then he nods at a wizened guy hovering around Becky. 'Who's that elderly android?'

'Ssh,' giggles Cathy. 'He's probably another of Becky's relations.' But it turns out he's the clerk, looking for Adam and Becky. They follow him through the door and a few minutes later, the door opens again and everyone else surges in to what looks like a small conference room with four rows of red-backed chairs. Adam and Becky turn around in the front row, smiling nervously at everyone. Becky's mum, nan and Mark sit with them; Adam signals to his mum and Reuben to join them but his mum, looking distinctly ill at ease, murmurs, 'We'll be all right here,' and she and Reuben sit alone in the back row.

Cathy has left a seat beside her for Jason. And when the door opens again, Cathy spins round and starts signalling. Just when she had given up hope of seeing him too. He's wearing a suit, blue shirt but no tie. He gives a quick wink to Adam, Becky and Mark, then saunters over to Cathy.

'Where have you been? I've been trying to contact you,' she asks.

'Sorry, things to do,' he flashes her a smile. Jez leans over. 'We were getting worried about you, mate.'

Jason half-smiles again. Then Lauren, who is sitting next to Jez, says, 'Hello Jason, how are you?'

'I'm all right.' His tone is not remotely friendly. Lauren immediately turns away.

Jason taps Cathy's hand. 'You look really nice.' She flushes with pleasure. She turns to face Jason. He's all dressed up and appears very handsome, only his eyes, his wonderful shiny eyes, have a horrifying emptiness about them. They don't blaze at you any more. Now they look all bleary and tired. Something's terribly wrong.

Jez nudges her. 'I think she's about to do the business.' He's pointing at a large, imposing woman who looks like a friendly headmistress. Adam and Becky get up and stand either side of her, then she introduces herself as the registrar and says, 'I'm delighted to welcome you all to the wedding of Adam and Becky . . .' She hands Becky the wedding certificate, 'And may I be the first to call you, Mrs Rosen,' she says, but before Becky can reply, the registrar is staring down at her watch, as if to say, 'Next'.

But for Becky, nothing can tarnish the magic of today. Everyone streams back outside and she and

Adam are enthusiastically pelted with confetti. They pose by the white Rolls Royce for Mark, while flash-bulbs explode all around them. 'I feel like I've just won the FA Cup final,' says Adam. There are more pictures of Becky showing off her wedding ring, which is gold with little diamonds.

The chauffeur is just opening the door for Adam and Becky when his mum and Reuben step forward. 'We won't stay for the reception but we wanted to be here,' she says.

'Thanks for coming, Mum, and you, Reuben.'

'Your father,' begins his mum, 'your father's also thinking about you today.'

Becky's mother joins them. 'They've done well, haven't they?' she says.

'Yes,' says Adam's mum. 'They both spoke up and . . .' her voice cracks a little, 'they look so grown-up, don't they?'

She puts an arm on Adam's shoulder. 'Look after Becky now, won't you. And Becky, keep an eye on him. He's a good lad really. Well, we won't keep you. Come on, Reuben.'

Adam watches them walk away. Then Becky squeezes his hand and whispers, 'All right?' Adam smiles at her, a smile that takes over his face. Everything that's happened to him has led to this moment; he cannot imagine living a minute without Becky now.

*

'And finally, we'd just like to thank you all for coming and sharing today with us.' Adam, sweating visibly, sits down to more applause. Both he and Becky wanted everyone seated around one round table, as they hated the idea of a top table and not-so-top tables. And he thinks the meal's gone really well. In fact there's such a good atmosphere, they even clapped his pathetic 'Thank you' speech. He's just relieved that's over.

The waitress is about to ask if anyone wants any more coffee when Mark springs up. 'Ladies and Gentlemen, and I think that includes everyone,' he gives his familiar dimpled smile, 'just before Adam and Becky leave for their honeymoon, I'd like you to raise your glasses to them, as we wish them lots of luck and happiness. To Adam and Becky.' Everyone, except Adam and Becky, get to their feet and the toast reverberates around the room.

Then Mark says, 'I've got one more toast, a bit of a special one. If you're popular, like me,' he grins around again, 'you make lots of mates. There's mates you have a laugh with, mates you go and see bands with, but friends, they're different, they're special. Now to have six true friends is pretty rare. But I have and they're all here. Only, this is the last time we're going to be together like this for quite a long time. Cathy and old Jez over there are going to Italy. Lauren's off to Birmingham tomorrow. I'm going to Sheffield next week.

And now, my main man, Jason, tells me that he's going away. We've been just a few roads away from each other for so long and suddenly, everything changes. So I'm going to ask them to stand up for this last toast: Cathy, Jez, Lauren, Adam, Becky and lastly Jason, who was our leader and incubated us all, really . . . come on, get up, don't be shy.' And all at once, the seven of them are up on their feet, grinning embarrassedly. Mark's voice rises. 'So! This toast is for us . . . FRIENDS FOR-EVER!'

He leaps forward and clinks glasses with Adam and Becky, next he runs down the table clinking glasses with Jason, Cathy, Lauren and Jez, repeating each time, 'Friends forever'. And then all seven of them are turning round and clinking glasses enthusiastically with each other.

Cathy turns to Jason, 'Friends forever', she whispers. 'Friends forever,' he repeats, gravely. She watches him repeat the toast to Jez, and then there's Lauren. Will he walk past her? But no, he doesn't. They mumble, 'Friends forever', without looking at each other.

When they finally sit down, Lauren's dad declares, 'What a performance,' and a waiter signals to Adam and Becky that their car is waiting to take them to the airport. There are more snatched goodbyes, Becky saving, to the very last, her mum and Mark. Mark kisses her, then whispers, 'The flowers . . . would you like me to give some of them to Thomas?' Becky can't reply, just hugs him as hard as she can. She and Adam finally slip away to tumultuous clapping and cheering.

'We ought to be going soon,' says Jez.

'But we've got lots of time yet,' says Cathy.

'Not really,' he replies. 'We've got to go to your house, pick up our cases, get a taxi to London, the tube to Heathrow, get our tickets . . .'

'All right,' interrupts Cathy. Jez, normally so laid-back, seems quite agitated and anxious. 'Just give me a few minutes, okay.' Then she notices Jason shaking hands with Mark. She rushes over to him. 'You're not going already, are you?' she asks.

'Yeah, I've got to be on my way.'

'So, how far are you going?'

'A long way, Cathy. Several galaxies away.'

'No, come on, tell me.' But he just gives her that same dead stare. His eyes are like a weary old man's. What's going on? She's got to know. She can't leave him like this.

'Jason, there's something wrong, isn't there?'

He hesitates, looks at her as if he'd like to tell her. But instead he says, 'I'm really pleased you are going to Venice with Jez. You deserve some happiness. Gallons and gallons of it.' Then, he kisses her. 'Take care of yourself,' he says and starts to walk away.

195

'But Jason,' she calls after him. 'You haven't told me where you're going. How can I write to you?'

He winks, 'Be lucky, now.'

'Jason, shall I send them to your home?' He doesn't answer. What is happening? Somehow, it's all to do with Lauren, isn't it?

And then, there is Lauren, gesturing in front of her. 'Jez says you're going in a minute.' She sounds breathless.

'Yes, that's right.'

'So we've got to talk, now.' Lauren starts pulling at her.

'Where are we going?'

'Need you ask,' says Lauren.

And of course, Cathy knows where they are going. How often has Lauren hissed, 'Got to talk to you, urgently,' and pulled her into the ladies. How many heart-to-hearts have they had in there?

This ladies is conveniently empty. Lauren looks around her. 'Brings back memories, doesn't it?'

'It sure does. So many traumas.'

'I know,' Lauren sighs dramatically. 'And you were always such a good listener, and gave such good advice. That's why I wanted us to say a proper goodbye . . .'

'Lauren,' says Cathy. 'Can I say something first?' She knows this is the one topic Lauren won't want to talk about. But she's got to tell her. 'I'm very

196

worried about Jason.' At once, Lauren stiffens. 'I think he's really unhappy and . . .'

'But what can I do? It's over.'

'No, it's not,' says Cathy, gently.

'Cathy, I should know.'

'It's not over for him,' says Cathy. 'And you – you must miss him.'

'I don't really miss men,' says Lauren, quickly.

'But he's talking about going away,' says Cathy. 'And he won't tell us where.'

'That's probably because he's not going anywhere,' says Lauren. 'We're all going away, so he has to say he is. He lives in a dream-world, anyway. He still thinks he's the flipping Lone Ranger, riding in to town on a black horse at sunset, riding out again at sunrise . . . Jason's so mixed up, Cathy. He really is and he's the most insecure person I've ever known.' She hesitates, 'He can also be the sweetest guy in the world, and he's not a user, like most men, I'll give him that. He's got his good side too, but,' she sighs heavily, 'I know you think I'm being a heartless bitch about Jason. Of course I still feel something for him. And one day I really hope we'll be friends – we're not even talking at the moment. He just cut me dead when I said hello to him today, which I did think was a bit childish but still . . . Jason does need someone. Only it's not me.' Suddenly, Cathy can feel this wild hope rising inside her as Lauren goes on. 'And I

197

wouldn't be helping Jason to pretend it was . . . But he will find someone else. I mean, he's not exactly ugly, is he?'

'No,' agrees Cathy. 'He's not ugly.' They both smile.

Lauren says, 'You do understand my position about Jason, don't you?'

'Yes,' says Cathy, slowly. 'I think I do.'

'Because I felt all this with Jason was driving a wedge between us. Sometimes you'd look at me like you hated me.'

'Oh, I didn't,' protests Cathy.

'Yes, you did. And that really upset me, my best friend . . .'

She's interrupted by Jez knocking on the door. 'Cathy, are you in there?'

'Yes, she is,' yells Lauren. 'And don't be so impatient. You've got her all to yourself for four months.' Then she turns back to Cathy. 'I wish you were coming to Birmingham with me,' she says softly. 'You will send me lots of exotic postcards, won't you?' Suddenly Lauren looks about six. Cathy's heart goes out to her.

'We're always going to be friends,' says Cathy. 'When I'm ninety, I'll bet I'll be ringing you up to go down the pub.'

'And I'll still be tarting myself up for hours beforehand . . .' They laugh and hug each other hard. Then, just as they used to, they link arms and walk back down the corridor.

'At last,' says Jez. He turns to Mark. 'They've been gabbling away in the ladies for ages.'

'Lauren, you're not leaving just yet, are you?' asks Mark. 'Your mum and dad are still here with my mum.'

'No I'll stay on with you.'

'Good,' says Mark, 'because everyone else is going. Now, Jason's gone.'

'Jason's gone,' repeats Cathy.

'But I think he's just going home,' says Mark. 'I don't think he's leaving yet, because earlier I heard him asking Adam if he could borrow his motorbike, so tonight I'll pop round and see him and . . .'

Cathy doesn't hear any more. Instead, deep inside her head she hears Jason saying to her, 'This guy drives himself and his motorbike over the cliff . . . that's the way I'll do it. There's Crompton Quarry . . . that'll be fine.' The words turn her icy cold.

No, wait, just because Jason's borrowing Adam's bike . . . she's being absurd, melodramatic. Then she thinks of him today, those sad, dead eyes, and the way he wouldn't say where he was going, just that it was several galaxies away. She shivers.

But there's no time to think anything else, because she's being rushed on. There are more noisy goodbyes, and then they are outside and Jez is saying, 'It would be bucketing down now,' and they are walking quickly down a road and everything seems so unreal. Cathy can't even remember where they are going until she sees the multi-storey car-park.

Now she is driving to her house and Jez is rubbing his hands and saying where they will be this time tomorrow and she is trying to smile. Outside, the rain pounds down, while the wind is hurling brightly-coloured but dead leaves up into the air. Some of them land, splat across the windscreen. But they can't cling on and are swept away into oblivion again. There's no time. No time, the windscreen wipers repeat the phrase over and over.

She pulls into her drive. 'We won't miss this weather, will we?' says Jez. He's been humming Italian songs to her all the way home. 'I can't wait to go now, can you?' he says.

'No,' says Cathy, flatly.

Inside, the house is empty, except for Scampi, who gives them his usual manic welcome. In the kitchen wait Jez's rucksack and her case. They'd decided to limit themselves to one case each, travel light, Jez said. She was hours packing hers and deciding what to take. Then neither she nor Jez could even lift it. She looks at the labels she'd stuck on her case and Jez's. They have rather a mournful air about them now, almost as if they know they're not going anywhere. Cathy starts. What makes her think that? Of course she's going.

'Shall we ring for a taxi and go right away?' says Jez.

'Yes. No, wait a minute,' says Cathy, putting on a light. 'It's so dark in here, isn't it. How about a quick cup of tea?'

'I'd rather just go,' says Jez. Then he adds, teasingly, 'You're not feeling a little homesick, are you?'

'No, it's not that,' says Cathy. 'It's just, I'm really worried about Jason and I feel I ought to do something.'

'What are you worried about?' asked Jez.

'I think he's really unhappy, needs someone.'

'Why don't you ring Mark, then,' says Jez. 'He'll be at the hotel, get him to go round and see Jason.'

'Yes, all right, I'll ring Mark,' says Cathy.

In a kind of trance, she walks to the hall and starts searching through the yellow pages for the hotel's number. Yes, there it is, Cartford 496282. So now, she'll ring Mark and tell him about Jason. He'll sort it out, won't he? He's Jason's best mate.

She starts dialling. 'Quick as you can,' murmurs Jez. He's literally breathing down her neck. Now the phone's ringing. Any second now she'll be put through to Mark and then she can leave Jason in safe hands . . . She slams the phone down. As she does this, her heart gives a massive thump as if in accompaniment. She slowly turns round. Jez is staring at her. 'What's wrong?' he asks.

'I can't do it,' her voice is barely above a whisper. 'I can't leave him,' she says. She tries to explain it to Jez, to herself. 'You see, Jason's helped me a lot in the past. I wrote to you about how he took the blame when I smashed that butcher's window. He's always been there for me . . .' But even as she's saying this, a loud voice inside her is crying, but that's not the only reason, is it? Say aloud the other reason, if you dare. Tell Jez the whole truth. Go on. You owe him that.

'You see, for years and years I've . . . and it's so crazy, because Jason's never once looked at me. Well, once he kissed me, that's all. But now, I feel that he really does need someone. Needs *me* and I've loved him for such a long time.' She stops. 'But I hate doing this, especially to you.'

Jez doesn't reply. He walks into the kitchen and picks up his rucksack. 'So that's that,' he says, casually. 'I'll just ring for a taxi, if you don't mind.'

'No, I'll take you, it's the least I can do.'

'I'd rather get a taxi, thanks,' says Jez. He goes into the hall. Cathy brushes away a tear. What has she done to Jez? But she thought she wanted to go away with him. Actually, the truth is, she never really thought about it at all. It was just an impulse. And every day since they'd said they'd go, she's been thinking not of Rome and Venice, but of

202

Jason, wondering how he's feeling, what he's doing, who he's with.

'Taxi will be here in three or four minutes,' says Jez, standing in the kitchen doorway.

'Jez I can't tell you how sorry I am,' begins Cathy. He turns away. 'You're really angry with me, aren't you?' says Cathy. 'You feel I've let you down.'

Jez shakes his head. 'Not really. I knew you wouldn't go. I sensed it all along. And then I saw the way you looked at Jason today. It was so obvious, I don't know why I didn't see it before.

'A few times I did suspect something. But today, that's why I was keen to rush you away. Still, Cathy do you really think . . . No, forget it.'

'Say it, please.'

'Do you really think Jason . . .' He hesitates again.

'Needs me,' prompts Cathy. 'I feel that he does. I feel it so strongly but . . . I could be totally wrong, couldn't I?'

Jez doesn't answer this. Outside a horn is sounded. 'That sounds like my cue,' says Jez.

'Can you ever forgive me?'

'Nothing to forgive. I guess we were both fooling ourselves really. A pity though. I could see you on a gondola in Venice, me serenading you.'

'So could I.'

'Ah well.' Jez picks up his rucksack. Cathy smiles

nervously, kisses him, says, 'Don't grow another beard, darling, because you look so much better without one. And don't take up smoking again, will you, that's what made you so ill and don't eat junk foods, have fresh fruit and vegetables . . .'

'You're worse than my mum. In fact, I'm pretty relieved you're not coming with me.'

'Lucky escape,' says Cathy, trying to smile.

'Too right.' The horn sounds again.

'I'd better go,' says Jez.

'You will write?'

'No, but I'll send you my address so you can write to me.'

'It's a deal,' says Cathy. She kisses him again. He gives her a wave. 'Please don't come out,' he says.

'Oh, all right. Take care, my darling. I hate to think of you going so far away.'

When Cathy's out of earshot, he murmurs, 'Me, far from you, impossible.'

Then Cathy runs to the window and waves his taxi off. Suddenly, she feels very alone. What if Jason's just borrowed Adam's bike to go for a spin? He's borrowed Adam's bike before. And what makes her so sure Jason wants her? Maybe he's got someone else. But she keeps coming back to those eyes. She peers outside. The darkness is pressing up tight against the window. Jason loves the dark, doesn't he? And if he is going to

Crompton Quarry, it'll probably be later tonight. But Cathy must get to him before then. She must act now.

She dials his number. She can't invite him round to her house because her mum and Giles will be back soon. She thinks, with sudden dread, of the explanations she's going to have to give them about not going to Italy. She'll invite him out for a drink. But she doesn't get the chance. For his mum answers and tells her Jason went out about twenty minutes ago and no, he didn't say where he was going, but he did tell her he wouldn't be in for dinner.

Just to allay the fear bubbling up inside her, she rings Adam's house. 'Hello, Mrs Rosen, it's Cathy. It was a lovely wedding, wasn't it?'

'Yes, Cathy, it was.' She says it firmly, like a lid snapping shut. Cathy shouldn't have rung her now. It's rude, intrusive. Mrs Rosen will want to be on her own. But Cathy's got to know.

'I'm sorry to bother you, Mrs Rosen. I just wanted to check – Jason hasn't been round, has he?'

'Well, yes he has,' she replies. 'In fact, you've just missed him, I'm afraid. He came round to borrow Adam's bike. I don't know where he was going but when he brings the bike back I can give him a message, if you like, Cathy – Cathy?' But Cathy's already rung off.

*

The motorbike explodes into life, its power charging through Jason. 'Yes, yes,' he cries, while the rain streams down his face. Familiar landscapes flash past for the last time. Now he's really flying along. But even now he can't leave it behind. It's still there, throbbing away in his head. That pain, that terrible pain.

Yet there was no way he could have missed Adam and Becky's wedding. Even though he knew Lauren would be swanning around there. And he knew too, that he'd spend days beforehand tormenting himself as he pictured Lauren saying, 'Jason, I think I've been too hasty. I want you back.' Four tiny little words: I want you back. It wouldn't have killed her to say them, would it? But of course, she didn't say them. SHE'LL NEVER SAY THEM.

A car horn howls behind him. Jason whirls round, raises two fingers and cries, 'Come and get me then. Come on. I don't care.'

He doesn't care because it's all over now. No, it isn't. You've got to go on, fight back. That's always been Jason's motto. Fight back. Hasn't he tried? Been out every night: at the sports centre, clubbing, parties, girls, getting legless, everything. Yet none of it worked. That horrible, grey emptiness never gave up its grip on him. Now it's eating its way right through him. Soon he'll have no insides left. Any second now they'll be blown away, because he's got nothing to hold on to, no one. It's all slipped away from him. Only oblivion lies ahead. But Jason's clever, he's getting out before that stop.

The rain rushes furiously into his face; it feels larger, heavier, more vicious, like hailstones. Now it's stinging, blinding. He can't even see where he's going any more. But Crompton Quarry lies ahead, he's sure of it.

It's a shame about Adam's motorbike. But Jason's left an envelope in his bedroom for Adam, it contains all his savings, more than enough for a new bike.

And when she hears about Jason tomorrow, will Lauren be sorry? Will she cry? Will she feel guilty? Of course she will. The rain lashes furiously against his face as he picks up speed. Lauren will sob her heart out or . . . Or will she just think, Crazy Jason strikes again. Yes, of course, that's all she'll think. She'd be right too. For it's not really her fault, is it? Come on, no more hiding, it's his fault, isn't it? All his fault. Crazy Jason, HIM! HIM! HIM! HIM!

The engine begins to scream.

Cathy screams, 'Jason!' then squelches her way frantically through the mud. She can see the motorbike rolled over on its side, right by the edge of the quarry, but Jason, where is he? She screams his name again and then she sees him, crouched a

207

few feet away from the bike, his hands over his face.

'Jason.'

He turns round very slowly. The rain hurls itself at him while he stumbles to his feet. He looks drenched to the skin. 'I meant to do it,' his voice is shaking. 'I was there, right on the edge.'

Cathy stares down. It's a great drop down to the stones and yellow mud below. She starts trembling.

'You know what I wish?' he demands. 'I wish I was a bloody island, that no one could ever find. Then you'd be safe, then no one could get to you.' He stops, and as if for the first time, takes in her presence. 'But what are you doing here?' he asks.

'I heard that you borrowed Adam's bike and somehow, I guessed . . .'

'No, no,' he interrupts. He looks dazed, bewildered now. 'But you're not here. You're going to Italy with Jez.'

'Jez went. I didn't. I couldn't.' Cathy hesitates for only a second. Go on, finish the sentence. Say it, finally. 'I couldn't leave you.'

He doesn't say anything, just stares, his eyes travelling over her, while Cathy takes in his blonde hair, his eyelashes, his perfectly shaped nose, his longish jaw. Then, suddenly, he reaches out and pulls her towards him. At once, Cathy feels herself surrounded by such tenderness, as he draws her closer and closer to him. He kisses her gently on the lips and says, 'You,' with such wonderment she gives a soft, little laugh.

'Yes, me, me all the time.' She reaches out and kisses him, a much longer kiss this time. His eyes look into hers, 'Cathy,' he whispers, as if he still can't believe it. Then he repeats her name and adds, 'You're getting soaked.' He gazes down at her legs which are just caked with mud, a smile playing about his lips. Cathy starts to smile too. Then Jason puts his arm around her. 'Let's go home,' he says.

Pete Johnson

ONE STEP BEYOND

Sometimes you're walking right on the edge and don't even realise it.

Like Alex. He's waited five years to take revenge on Mr Stones.

And Natasha. She's always done what her parents tell her – until the day she turns sixteen.

Then there's Yorga. He has a brilliant idea to stop the hated Casuals taking over his town.

Just three of the people who don't realise they're right on the edge – until they take one step beyond.

A collection of eight dazzling stories of love, revenge, laughter and horror by the author of the *Friends Forever* series.

Also by Pete Johnson

I'D RATHER BE FAMOUS

'I don't want to just fade away down some back street, with Adam, and then end up on a gravestone with no one remembering who I am. I want to make my mark, show everyone I'm here and sign at least a few autographs before I die.'

Jade is sixteen and a half, with a steady boyfriend called Adam and a sometime job selling videos. But it isn't enough. Jade's problem is that she has very little talent, but she knows she can be a TV presenter. All she needs is one lucky break. Then Jade hears a dating show is looking for applicants. Adam would go crazy if she ever applied. So dare she? Jade dares . . . and her life will never be quite the same again.

A warm, funny and touching story which looks at television fame and teenage life today with real understanding.

'Very entertaining.'

The Indy

'Well researched, enjoyable and easy to relate to.'
Material Matters

A selected list of titles available from Teens

While every effort is made to keep prices low, it is sometimes necessary to increase prices at short notice. Mandarin Paperbacks reserves the right to show new retail prices on covers which may differ from those previously advertised in the text or elsewhere.

The prices shown below were correct at the time of going to press.

☐	7497 0095 5	**Among Friends**	Caroline B Cooney	£2.99
☐	7497 0145 5	**Through the Nightsea Wall**	Otto Coontz	£2.99
☐	7497 0582 5	**The Promise**	Monica Hughes	£2.99
☐	7497 0171 4	**One Step Beyond**	Pete Johnson	£2.50
☐	7497 0281 8	**The Homeward Bounders**	Diana Wynne Jones	£2.99
☐	7497 0312 1	**The Changeover**	Margaret Mahy	£2.99
☐	7497 0473 X	**Shellshock**	Anthony Masters	£2.99
☐	7497 0323 7	**Silver**	Norma Fox Mazer	£3.50
☐	7497 0325 3	**The Girl of his Dreams**	Harry Mazer	£2.99
☐	7497 0280 X	**Beyond the Labyrinth**	Gillian Rubinstein	£2.50
☐	7497 0558 2	**Frankie's Story**	Catherine Sefton	£2.50
☐	7497 0009 2	**Secret Diary of Adrian Mole**	Sue Townsend	£2.99
☐	7497 0333 4	**Plague 99**	Jean Ure	£2.99
☐	7497 0147 1	**A Walk on the Wild Side**	Robert Westall	£2.99

All these books are available at your bookshop or newsagent, or can be ordered direct from the publisher. Just tick the titles you want and fill in the form below.

Mandarin Paperbacks, Cash Sales Department, PO Box 11, Falmouth, Cornwall TR10 9EN.

Please send cheque or postal order, no currency, for purchase price quoted and allow the following for postage and packing:

UK including BFPO
£1.00 for the first book, 50p for the second and 30p for each additional book ordered to a maximum charge of £3.00.

Overseas including Eire
£2 for the first book, £1.00 for the second and 50p for each additional book thereafter.

NAME (Block letters) ....

ADDRESS ....

....

☐ I enclose my remittance for ....

☐ I wish to pay by Access/Visa Card Number

Expiry Date